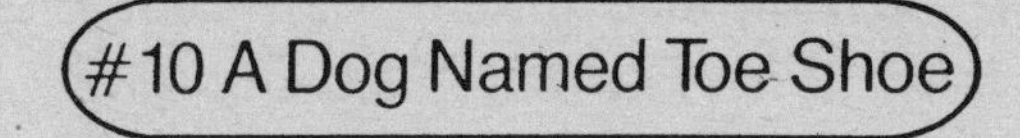
#10 A Dog Named Toe Shoe

Look for these books
in the Bad News Ballet series:

1 *The Terrible Tryouts*
2 *Battle of the Bunheads*
3 *Stupid Cupids*
4 *Who Framed Mary Bubnik?*
5 *Blubberina*
6 *Save D.A.D.!*
7 *The King and Us*
8 *Camp Clodhopper*
9 *Boo Who?*
#10 *A Dog Named Toe Shoe*

#10 A Dog Named Toe Shoe

Jahnna N. Malcolm

SCHOLASTIC INC.
New York Toronto London Auckland Sydney

Special thanks to: Leah Rice, Josh Sanitate, Chelle Snook, Chad Lewis, Jason Ostrowski, Cory Meade, Jessie Vollin, Abby Coleman.

ISBN 0-590-43398-9

12 11 10 9 8 7 6 5 4 3 2 1 1 2 3 4 5 6/9

Printed in the U.S.A. 40

First Scholastic printing, February 1991

For
Frank The Wonder Dog
1977–1990

Chapter One

"I'm freezing!" Kathryn McGee pulled her long, red-and-white knit scarf up over her nose so that only her green eyes peeked out. "It must be below zero."

The skinny sixth-grader huddled with her three friends on the marble steps in front of the Deerfield Academy of Dance, while a chilly winter wind swirled around them.

"What are you complaining about?" Gwendolyn Hays grumbled between chattering teeth. "At least you're wearing that thick down jacket and jeans." The chubby redhead gestured to her bare legs, which were starting to look blotchy in the freezing Ohio cold. Instead of warm winter boots, she had black patent leather shoes on her feet, with white cotton anklets. "Mom made me wear a dress today 'cause everyone in my Young Charmers group was *supposed* to have our picture taken today."

"Young Charmers?" McGee repeated. "You're kidding."

"No, I'm not. It's a new mother-and-daughter group Mother formed with some ladies at the country club," Gwen explained with a groan. "She tried to get your mom to join, but your mom said you'd never go for it."

"She was right," McGee said shortly.

Gwen and McGee's mothers were close friends, and the two girls had met several years before when they were forced to attend a mother-daughter luncheon.

"I wish I could quit," Gwen added. "But Mom is the president, and I'm her only daughter."

"So how did the group picture come out?"

"It didn't. The snow was so bad, the stupid photographer couldn't get out of his driveway, and I've had to look like this for a whole day." Gwen tugged at the pink bow pinned to the side of her limp red curls. Normally her hair hung in a straight pixie cut, but that morning her mother had insisted on curling it. "I feel like a poodle."

"Well, consider yourself lucky that your hair isn't like that all the time," Mary Bubnik drawled in her Oklahoma accent. She patted the tight ringlets of golden hair that hung around her head. Over her curls she wore a pair of pink earmuffs that had little cat faces embroidered on them. "*My* hair is always curly, and it's *bo*-ring."

"Couldn't we wait inside the Academy?" Zan Reed asked in her soft voice. The tall, thin black girl had been standing with her hands shoved in the pockets of her wool coat. "I've lost all feeling in my fingers."

McGee shook her head. "When Rocky called me, she said she had horrible news, and that we had to meet *outside* the dance studio. She didn't want the Bunheads to know anything about it."

"Bunheads" was the name the gang had given the snobby girls in their ballet class. Courtney Clay and her friends Page Tuttle and Alice Wescott wore their hair in tight little buns on top of their heads and never let the gang forget that they were the best dancers in their class.

"If Rocky doesn't get here soon," Mary Bubnik said, "all she'll find is four lil' ice cubes with us frozen inside."

"My legs are two frozen stumps, my poodle curls have little icicles hanging from them, and — " Gwen ran one of her mittens across her face and sniffed loudly. "And now my nose is running."

"I wonder what's keeping Rocky?" Zan murmured, hunching over to keep her face out of the freezing wind.

"I don't know," McGee replied as she jogged in a tiny circle to keep warm. "But Rocky was really upset when I talked to her. I've never heard her sound like that."

"Maybe she's gotten in trouble at her school," Zan suggested. Rochelle Garcia had a reputation for being tough, and more than once had gotten in a fight with some bully on the playground.

"Yeah," Gwen agreed. "Maybe she and Russell Stokes went at it again."

McGee shook her head. "Rocky said this was the worst thing that had ever happened to her."

"Then it couldn't be Russell Stokes," Mary Bubnik remarked. "I think Rocky likes fighting with him." The previous spring Rocky and Russell had gotten in a fight, but they had made up and even gone to the mall for a Coke.

Zan checked her watch. "Ballet class starts in five minutes. We need time to get dressed. What should we do?"

Gwen, whose wire-rimmed glasses had fogged up, blinked at the group and declared, "I say we wait for Rocky."

"What do you mean, wait?" McGee spun to face Gwen. "Geez Louise, you're the one who's suffering from terminal frostbite."

"I'm also suffering from extreme dance-itis."

Mary Bubnik looked puzzled. "What's that mean?"

"It mean's I'm allergic to ballet lessons," Gwen explained, polishing her glasses on the hem of her dress. "Every time Mrs. Bruce starts playing that dance music, my feet go berserk and I do all the wrong steps."

Zan checked her watch again. "I really think we should go to class. Then, if Rocky comes, we'll talk about her problem afterwards."

"Wait a minute!" McGee held up a gloved hand. "I thought I heard something. Something weird."

The girls froze in place and cocked their heads alertly. The only sound came from their own breathing as big steamy clouds puffed out of their mouths into the frosty air.

Finally Mary Bubnik, who had lifted one earmuff to listen, said, "I think I hear it, too. It's coming from around the corner of the building."

McGee shut her eyes in concentration. "You're right. And it sounds like someone crying."

"Crying!" The four girls looked at each other and gasped, "Rocky!"

All thoughts of the cold or being late for class vanished from their minds as the girls raced for the side of the building. Rocky was in trouble and she needed their help.

McGee was the first to round the corner. She froze in her tracks. The alley was deserted except for a couple of metal trash cans that were under a rusty fire escape. "I don't see her anywhere."

"But where did the crying come from?" Zan asked.

Gwen shrugged. "It must have just been the wind."

Mary Bubnik, who had wandered over to the trash

cans, suddenly put her mittened hands to her mouth and gasped, "Oh, you guys, come look!"

They raced to Mary Bubnik's side, afraid that they might find Rocky lying there hurt, or worse. Instead, sitting behind the metal trash cans in the icy alley was the strangest-looking animal any of them had ever seen.

"He's beautiful!" Mary Bubnik gasped.

Gwen cried at the same time, "He's so ugly!"

"What *is* he?" Zan asked.

"He's a dog, silly." Mary knelt down and held out the back of her hand. "Come here, boy, I won't hurt you."

The dog had long funny ears that stuck out to the side. He blinked his liquid brown eyes at Mary solemnly as he thumped his tail against the side of the garbage can.

"Come on," Mary Bubnik urged, making little clucking sounds with her mouth.

Slowly the dog pulled himself to his feet and moved out of the shadows.

"This guy is two dogs long and half a dog high," McGee said in amazement.

"His head looks kind of like a Saint Bernard's with long gremlin ears," Gwen said.

"But his body is definitely like a wiener dog's," McGee added. "Or one of those basset hounds."

Zan giggled. "He's like a basset hound and a Saint Bernard combined."

"A Saint Bernasset," Gwen joked.

"He has velvet ears." Mary ruffled the fur on the dog's head and cooed, "And be-*yew*-tiful eyes."

The mournful hound raised his big head and without warning, gave Mary Bubnik a big sloppy kiss with his pink tongue. Mary fell backward in the snow, giggling. "He likes me!"

"Dog kisses are disgusting," Gwen muttered. "You don't know anything about him. He could be carrying all kinds of diseases."

Mary wrapped her arm around the dog's thick neck. "He doesn't have a collar so he must be a stray." She scratched him gently behind one ear. "Was that you crying?"

The dog answered her with a soft whimper, and Mary looked up at the others, her eyes wide with concern. "The poor boy is so cold, and I bet he's starving, too. Does anybody have any food?"

All of them turned to Gwen, who clutched her blue dance bag to her chest. "Why's everybody staring at me?"

"Come on, Gwen." McGee put her hands on her hips. "I'm sure you must have at least two packs of Twinkies in there, plus a couple of bags of M&M's and Ho-Hos. Now fork 'em over."

Gwen clutched the bag even tighter to her chest. "These are for emergencies."

"This *is* an emergency," Mary cried. "Can't you see this doggie is starving to death?"

Gwen saw the accusing looks on her friends' faces and reluctantly opened the top of her bag. "Well, maybe I have *something* he can eat." She pulled out a package of Twinkies and carefully removed one snack cake.

McGee punched her in the arm. "Don't be stingy, Hays. Give him both."

"Why do I always have to be the one to give up my food?" Gwen grumbled as she handed Mary Bubnik the whole package.

"Because you're the one who always *has* food," Zan pointed out logically.

Mary Bubnik took the cakes and held them out one at a time to the strange basset hound. He sniffed carefully and then took one of the cakes out of her hand.

"There you go, Oscar," Mary said. "Eat it. It's good for you."

"Oscar!" McGee repeated. "How do you know his name is Oscar?"

"I don't. It's just that my Uncle Oscar has big brown eyes—"

"Does he have floppy ears and big feet, too?" Gwen cut in.

"No, but Uncle Oscar has been awfully nice to me since my parents got divorced," Mary explained. "So I'm naming this doggie after him."

"Oscar." Gwen shook her head in disgust. "What a dumb name."

"Don't listen to her, boy," Mary Bubnik whispered, handing the dog the other snack cake. This time he swallowed it in one gulp.

"Look how smart he is." McGee pointed at the dog, who was staring at Gwen intently. "He knows you have more food, and he wants it."

"Well, he can't have it," Gwen said, holding the bag over her head. "And if he's so smart, he can just go buy his own food."

"How can you say that?" Mary Bubnik protested, burying her face in the dog's furry neck.

"Yes," Zan said, kneeling beside Mary and wrapping her arms about the dog protectively. "He's destitute, and doesn't have a home or any money. And he's cold." She stroked the top of his head. "Aren't you, boy."

As if in answer to Zan's words, the dog let out two quiet little whimpers and nuzzled her hand.

"Look, I thought we were supposed to go to dance class," Gwen said, backing away to the edge of the alley. "If we stand around here any longer, we might as well forget the whole thing and go home."

"Gwen's right," McGee said. "I'll bet Rocky thought it was too cold to wait outside and has been in the warm dressing room all along."

"You really think she's at the studio?" Zan asked.

McGee nodded. "I'd bet money on it."

"Then what are we waiting for?" Gwen cried. "Let's go."

Mary Bubnik stood up. "But what are we going to do about Oscar?"

McGee twirled the end of one braid slowly around her finger. "Maybe he *does* have a home, and he just lost his collar or something."

"In which case we should just leave him here," Gwen said.

"Leave him?" Mary wailed. "But he's so cold!"

"If he stays behind the trash cans," Zan said, "he'll be out of the wind. And now that Gwen's given him her Twinkies, we know he's not hungry."

"Did you see how fast he ate that last Twinkie?" Mary retorted. "I think he's still hungry."

"Gwen, give him some more food so we can go inside," McGee ordered.

"No." Gwen shook her head stubbornly.

McGee snatched the dance bag out of Gwen's hands. "Sorry, but if you don't give him something else, we're all going to freeze to death."

She opened the top of Gwen's blue canvas bag with the pink toe shoes sewn on the side and peered inside. "I don't believe it."

"What?"

"You've got an entire candy store in here." McGee started tossing candy bars, cookies, and bags of M&M's onto the icy concrete. The dog snapped them up the moment they hit the ground.

"See, Oscar was starved!" Mary exclaimed.

"I'll say he was," McGee said. "He's even eating the candy wrappers."

"What a pig!" Gwen wrinkled her nose in disgust, then turned to McGee and snapped, "And you're a thief!" She yanked the bag back. "That was my lunch for all of next week."

"Your mom lets you take candy for lunch?" McGee exclaimed.

"Of course not. But this is Earth Week at my school, and the cafeteria's only serving health food made of all sorts of weird stuff like seaweed and soy meal and oat bran." Gwen made a sour face. "It all tastes like cardboard."

Zan checked her watch again. "Our dance class begins in less than one minute. If we're going to talk to Rocky, we have to leave now."

McGee patted Mary Bubnik on the shoulder. "Come on, Mary. Oscar will wait for you. It's only an hour."

Mary wrapped her pink knit scarf around the dog's neck, then took her little cat earmuffs off her head and slipped them over the dog's ears. "Here, Oscar, these will keep you warm. I'll be back in no time at all." She gave him one last squeeze, then hurried out of the alley with the others toward the Deerfield Academy of Dance.

McGee led the girls through the big glass doors of Hillberry Hall and up the three flights of stairs to the ballet academy.

"I hope he's here when we get back," Mary Bubnik said as they paused for breath on the second landing.

"Don't worry," McGee replied confidently. "He'll be there. I'm sure of it."

"How can you be so sure?" Mary asked.

"Because if you were a dog and some girl put kitty earmuffs on you, would you go out in public?"

Mary smiled sheepishly. "You've got a point."

Zan threw open the door to the Academy office just as the first piano chords were being played in studio B. "Uh-oh. We've got a big problem."

"What?" Gwen huffed as she staggered into the office.

"Class is already starting, and we're not even dressed."

The girls dashed for the dressing room to change into their leotards and tights. The important news Rocky had to tell them would have to wait.

Chapter Two

The gang spent the next forty-five minutes of class watching the door, hoping to see Rocky come through it. She hadn't been in the dressing room and hadn't made it to class.

"I hope she's not hurt or something," Mary Bubnik whispered as their teacher led them through the *adagio* in the middle of the floor.

The music and movements were slow, and it was hard for the dancers to keep their balance. As Gwen strained to hold her leg in an *arabesque,* she murmured, "Rocky's the lucky one. She's probably out having a pizza while we're in here getting leg cramps."

McGee squinted at the little alarm clock sitting on

the edge of the piano where Mrs. Bruce, the accompanist, was dramatically tinkling the keys. "Only fifteen more minutes and we can go hunt for her."

"This final step is called *pas de chat,*" their teacher Annie Springer announced as the *adagio* finished.

"*Pas de chat* means 'the step of the cat,' " Annie explained. "And it looks like a cat leaping over a fence sideways." The pretty, dark-haired teacher demonstrated by jumping to the right and raising her knees high in the air.

Gwen narrowed her eyes in concentration and tried it. She sucked in her plump stomach as best she could and sprang sideways, landing with a loud "thunk-thunk" on the floor.

"That sounded like the step of the elephant," Courtney Clay cracked just loudly enough for the rest of the class to overhear.

"Well, what do you expect from a hippo like her?" Page hissed back.

Gwen's face turned a fluorescent pink color, but she didn't say anything. Her weight was a very touchy subject. She just put her head down and moved to the far side of the room.

Mary Bubnik leaned her head close to Zan's ear. "I wish Rocky were here," she whispered. "She wouldn't have let Courtney get away with saying that. Rocky would have given her a karate chop right between the eyes."

Rocky had studied karate and, on more than one

occasion, had threatened to use it on Courtney when the Bunhead had gotten too obnoxious.

"That was pretty good, Gwen," Annie called. "Next time, try to land on the balls of your feet."

Gwen slumped against the *barre* at the far end of the studio and muttered, "There's not going to be a next time."

Because it was called "the step of the cat," Mary Bubnik instinctively held her hands in front of her like paws. Courtney and the others snickered loudly as they watched Mary, who was all gangly arms and knobby knees, hop sideways across the floor. Even their teacher giggled.

"That's very cute, Mary," Annie said, hiding a smile behind her fingers. "And it might even be a way we could use the step in a ballet about alley cats. But for this class, try to hold one arm to the side with the other curved in front of you, and keep your knees turned out."

"That's a lot to remember," Mary Bubnik said pleasantly. "But I'll try."

Zan was dreading having to cross the floor alone, especially with Courtney and the Bunheads making cracks about everybody. So when her turn came she just put her head down and danced as fast as she could towards the far corner of the room.

"The step looked very nice, Zan," Annie called. "But next time, try to keep in time with the music."

McGee and a girl named Darcy did their steps

across the floor together, and Annie applauded when they were done. "Very good, you two. Just try to get your knees up a little bit higher next time, and don't look down at the floor."

Courtney went next and executed the step perfectly, smiling at her own reflection in the big mirrors lining one side of the studio. Alice and Page followed right behind her, springing lightly in the air.

"I can't think of a more perfect step for them," McGee muttered, watching the three Bunheads hop in unison.

"Yeah, they're the cattiest people I know," Gwen quipped. The rest of the gang laughed, and Gwen felt a little better.

When every girl in the class had taken a turn, Annie Springer clapped her hands together and called, "Very good, girls. Now we still have ten minutes left of class, so gather round — I have an announcement to make."

"You're getting married!" Mary Bubnik cried with glee as all of the students sat cross-legged on the wooden floor around their teacher.

Annie, who had perched on a small stool with her black dance skirt nearly touching the floor, threw back her head and laughed. "No! Not *that* kind of announcement. This is about the Ballet."

Courtney Clay shot her hand in the air. "I know what it is. My mother told me." She smiled smugly at the room.

Courtney's mother was on the board of directors of the Deerfield Ballet, and Courtney never let anyone forget how important she was.

Annie folded her hands in her lap. "Well, then, Courtney, do you want to tell the class the news?"

"The Winter Carnival is Deerfield's biggest event of the season," Courtney explained. "With the ice-sculpting contests, and the sled races, and the Scandinavian food festivals, it's attracting more and more people every year from all over the state. *Well* — " She took a deep breath. "This year, the Ballet and the Academy have agreed to participate."

"That's right," Annie said. "Mr. Anton has staged a ballet especially for the occasion. It will be performed on the big stage at the end of Lake Deerfield, and it's called *Les Patineurs.*"

"Lay Patty Nooers?" Mary Bubnik repeated. "What's that?"

"It's French for *The Skaters,*" Annie explained. Her cheeks flushed lightly as she added, "And I'll be dancing the lead role of Marie Chevreau."

"Oh, you'll be truly wonderful!" Zan gushed. "I just know it."

Annie Springer was the prima ballerina with the Deerfield Ballet. She had danced the role of the Sugar Plum Fairy in *The Nutcracker,* and the girls had fallen in love with her. She was not only a lovely dancer, but a very sweet person.

"But here's the best part." Annie leaned forward

and lowered her voice dramatically. "All of the dancers from the Academy will be in the show, too, because we are staging a huge extravaganza on ice."

"Ice?" Gwen gulped. "We have to *dance* on ice?"

"She can't even dance on a wooden floor," Page drawled sarcastically. "How is she going to dance on ice?"

A flurry of giggles ran around the group and Annie said quickly, "Let me explain. Most of you won't really be dancing. You'll be part of the costume parade that crosses the ice on sleds."

Mary Bubnik clapped her hands together. "That sounds like fun!"

"Of course, those of you who can skate will be dressed in wonderful costumes and lead the sleds."

"McGee, you're a fabulous skater," Gwen said. "You could be the lead skater."

McGee smiled proudly. She had been skating for as long as she could remember, and was a member of the Fairview Express, the hottest junior ice hockey team around. They'd been champions of their league for the last two years in a row.

"There's even a contest being sponsored by the Ballet for best individual sled decoration," Annie said. "That should really get everyone in Deerfield involved."

"Hey," McGee said, "my Dad has an old American Flyer that we could use."

"And my parents would let us use their art supplies

to decorate it," Zan added enthusiastically. Her parents were both artists, and taught at the Deerfield Art Institute.

"When does all this take place?" McGee asked, raising her hand.

"Next Saturday," Annie replied.

"Next week?" Gwen squeaked. "How are we going to decorate a sled and be in an extravaganza in that short a time?"

Annie laughed. "We're having a meeting for all of those who wish to participate in the parade. It will be Monday morning, here at the Academy."

"But what about school?" Mary Bubnik asked.

"That's President's Day," Courtney said. "Remember? We don't have any school. My sled is finished, but I'll be using that day to put a few personal touches on it."

"Not fair," Gwen grumbled. "She knew about the contest way before anyone else."

Courtney patted her bun. "That's because my mother's on the board, and yours isn't."

"Big deal," McGee said. "We can beat you in that contest with our eyes closed."

"Try it," Courtney said with a superior smile. "Just try it."

Annie cleared her throat loudly to get their attention and the girls quieted down instantly. "Now Monday morning we will be handing out costumes for the parade. It's very important that you arrive on time or you won't get a costume. Remember, be here at ten a.m. It should be a lot of fun!"

Several girls in the class cheered.

Annie gestured for Mrs. Bruce to play, and then she said, "Page, will you lead us in the final curtsey?"

"I'd be happy to," Page replied, flouncing up to the front of the class. The blonde-haired girl stepped to the side and, raising her arms in a lovely oval around her face, tucked one leg behind the other in a deep bow. The rest of the class followed suit. As they bent low, McGee caught Courtney's eye and couldn't resist sticking her tongue out at her.

The gang hurried out of the classroom toward the dressing room while the rest of the girls lingered in the studio chatting excitedly about the Winter Carnival. McGee threw back the black curtain covering the door to the dressing room and gasped in dismay.

Sitting in the dark on one of the far benches was Rocky Garcia. She was in her red satin jacket and jeans and sat hunched over, staring at her high-top tennis shoes. Her thick black hair seemed to explode from underneath the gray stocking cap that had been pulled tightly over her ears.

"Rocky?" McGee whispered.

Rocky raised her head and in the half-light the girls could see that her eyes were red from crying. She sniffed loudly and looked back down at her feet.

"Has something happened?" Zan asked.

Rocky nodded. "My dad got the word today from the base commander."

"He's been fired?" Gwen said, stepping into the room.

"No. Worse." Rocky kicked at the wooden floor with the toe of her red sneaker. "He's been transferred."

Chapter Three

"You're moving?" McGee gasped. "I don't believe it!"

"Dad broke it to us last night." Rocky sighed heavily and leaned her head back against the wall. "When we came to Ohio, my dad promised me and my brothers that we'd be staying here for a long time. I thought I'd finally get to stay at a school more than one year."

Rocky and her four brothers lived with her parents on Curtiss-Dobbs Air Force Base, just outside of Deerfield. Sergeant Garcia was constantly being transferred and had to go wherever the Air Force sent him. Rocky had spent the last six years of her life in seven different schools. It seemed as if her family was always living out of a suitcase.

"Now it looks like we have to pack up and move again," Rocky grumbled.

"You're moving?" Courtney Clay called merrily from the curtained door. "Let me know when, and I'll throw you a going-away party." She paused and, with a smug glance over her shoulder at Page and Alice, added, "The day *after* you leave."

The Bunheads burst out giggling and McGee snapped, "Courtney, why don't you go soak your head."

Courtney ignored her and breezed past McGee over to the dressing table with the big mirror. She picked up a brush and carefully smoothed a stray hair or two that had escaped from her bun during dance class. Page and Alice gathered their clothes and began dressing beside their leader.

None of the gang said anything while the rest of the girls in the class shuffled into the dressing room to change out of their leotards. They were still numb with shock from Rocky's news. Finally Mary Bubnik sat down beside Rocky and whispered, "When *do* you have to move?"

"Dad said it may be the end of this month."

"Oh, no!" McGee groaned. "That's too soon."

"I don't know what we'll do without you," Mary Bubnik said, trying to keep her chin from quivering.

"Where do you have to go?" Zan asked, silently hoping that it wasn't someplace far away.

Rocky tugged her stocking cap off her head and slapped it against her leg. "It looks like it's going to be some base in Nebraska."

"Nebraska?" Gwen wrinkled her nose. "That's halfway across the world."

"You're telling me," Rocky grumbled.

"How can your father make you move in the middle of the school year?" Zan complained. "That's truly *awful.*" Being a shy person, Zan knew how difficult it was to make new friends — and she'd lived in the same town her entire life.

McGee, who had slipped her jeans on over her leotard and tights, slammed her fist against the bank of lockers standing against the wall. "You can't move," she said flatly. "That's all there is to it!"

"How are you going to stop her?" Gwen called from behind the freestanding mirror where she was changing her clothes.

"I'll just go talk to the head guy on the Air Force base," McGee replied. "Maybe he'll listen to reason." She faced Rocky. "What's his name?"

"Colonel Corbin is the base commander," Rocky said without looking up.

"Then I'll talk to Colonel Corbin."

"I'm sure he's going to listen to some sixth-grader," Gwen said, stepping out from behind the mirror. "You won't get past his secretary. They probably won't even let you on the base."

"Well, have you got a better idea?" McGee demanded.

"Yes." Gwen shoved her wire-rimmed glasses up on her nose and looked at Rocky. "When your family goes to Nebraska, you can stay with me and finish out the year at my school."

Mary Bubnik clapped her hands together. "What a great idea! Then we could see you all the time. And when summer comes, you can stay with me. My mom would love it."

"I'm sure my parents would let you stay with me for a while, too," Zan chimed in enthusiastically.

"And then next year, you can come live with me and go to my school," McGee finished.

Rocky smiled sadly. "But what about my mom and dad, and my brothers?"

"I thought you hated your brothers," Gwen said.

"I do," Rocky said. "But I could never live away from them. I'd miss them too much."

"But what about us?" Mary Bubnik asked in a small voice. "Won't you miss us?"

Rocky sprang to her feet. "Don't be a jerk," she said roughly. "Of course I'll miss you. Why do you think I'm so upset?"

"Oh, puh-*leeeze!*" Courtney Clay said, stuffing her brush in her dance bag. "This is making me sick.

Go ahead and move, see if I care." She looped her bag over her shoulder and headed for the dressing room door. "We've got more important things to worry about."

"Like the Winter Carnival," Page added.

"And planning our winning sled entry," Alice Wescott finished, as she and Page followed Courtney out of the room.

After the girls had left, Mary turned to Rocky and said, "I can think of only one thing good about moving to Nebraska."

"What's that?" Rocky asked.

"The Bunheads won't be there."

Gwen slipped her coat on and struggled to close it over her pudgy stomach. "I hate to break it to you, Mary, but there are Bunheads everywhere. They're not always as obvious as Courtney and Page, but they're there just the same."

"That's all the more reason to stay," McGee declared. "At least you *know* these Bunheads."

The girls pulled on the rest of their winter gear and shuffled out of the studio and down the three flights of stairs in silence. At the bus stop, the gang huddled together in a tight group, shielding their faces from the cold.

Rocky suddenly hit herself on the head. "I was so upset about the move that I missed my bus this morning, and now I nearly forgot to tell you about my slumber party."

"Party?" Mary Bubnik asked. "When?"

"Tomorrow night." Rocky tugged on her stocking cap. "Mom said since it was a holiday, and because we have to move, I deserve a treat."

"That sounds like fun," Zan said, trying to sound enthusiastic after the bad news.

"It would be the perfect time to work on our decorations for the Ice Extravaganza," McGee added.

"Great!" Gwen said. "I'll bring my brother's sled."

"Whoa! Time out!" Rocky said, putting her hands in the shape of a "T." "What extravaganza? And what sled contest?"

For a second the girls put aside their sadness about Rocky's leaving, and they all talked excitedly about the upcoming Carnival.

"We're all going to be part of a big parade that crosses the ice," Zan explained.

Mary nodded. "And we'll have costumes and everything."

"Of course Courtney has the jump on us in the sled-decorating contest, but we can beat her," McGee said firmly. "I'm sure of it!"

"When is this thing?" Rocky asked.

"It's real soon," Mary Bubnik said. "Next Saturday."

Rocky blew on her hands. "I don't think I can be in it. If this move is like the others, I'll probably be too busy packing to come. Mom may even make me drop out of dance class early."

"Oh, Rocky, this is terrible," Mary Bubnik said, her eyes filling with tears. "Don't even think that."

"There's got to be some way to stop this transfer," McGee muttered. She cocked her head and asked, "Do orders ever get changed?"

Rocky squinted one eye in thought. "Sometimes. A neighbor of ours on the base in Florida was all set to go to California, but the orders changed the day before they were supposed to move."

"What happened?" Zan asked.

"They were sent to Germany."

"Germany!" Mary Bubnik gasped. "That's way too far away. We'd *never* see you."

"Don't worry, we're not being sent to Germany," Rocky reassured her.

"Nebraska might as well be Germany," Gwen said as she dug into her dance bag and pulled out a bag of M&M's. Tearing off the top of it with her teeth, she poured half the bag into her mouth and mumbled, "We're never going to see you again."

Zan shook her head. "This is truly a disaster."

"You guys quit getting so sappy and *think*," McGee barked angrily. "There's got to be a way we can get Colonel Corbin to change Rocky's orders."

"Maybe if we wrote him a letter," Mary suggested, "and explained to him that Rocky has to stay because the ballet school needs her."

Rocky rolled her eyes. "I'm sure."

"If you were one of the scholarship students," Zan said thoughtfully, "it might be more convincing."

"How does she get to be one of them?" Gwen asked.

"Miss Jo and Mr. Anton hold auditions," Zan replied, "and they judge on aptitude, enthusiasm, and promise."

"That's out," Rocky said, shoving her hands in the pocket of her satin jacket. "I can't even spell aptitude, I have zero enthusiasm about ballet, and I never make a promise I can't keep."

"This is too depressing," Gwen mumbled, as she finished off the bag of M&M's in one more gulp. She crumpled the bag in her hand and tossed it in the wastebasket. "I think we need to have a snack."

McGee stared at Gwen in amazement. "How can you think about food at a time like this?"

"It's times like these that make me the most hungry," Gwen answered matter-of-factly.

"But you just inhaled that entire bag of M&M's."

"Right," Gwen replied. "And now I'm thirsty. I say we get out of the cold and have some hot chocolate or something."

"What do you say, Rocky?" Mary Bubnik asked.

"Gee, I don't know." Rocky watched the city bus come lumbering down the street toward their stop. "I told my parents I'd come home right after class."

"But you're moving," Mary Bubnik pointed out.

"This may be one of the last times that we'll all be together."

"Mary's right," McGee agreed. "Stay with us a little longer."

The bus pulled up to the stop and the brakes squeaked and exhaled a loud gush of air. Then the driver slid open the door.

Rocky hesitated, looking first at her friends, then back at the open door.

"Are you getting on, or not?" the driver demanded. "I don't have all day, and the cold air's coming in."

"Come on, Rocky," McGee pleaded. "Stay."

Rocky wavered for one more second, then stepped back. "I'm staying."

"Kids," the driver snorted in disgust. The door swung shut with a loud hiss, and the bus pulled away from the curb. For the first time, the gang saw a grin crease Rocky's face. "Okay, where should we go now?"

"Hi Lo's!" Gwen sang out happily. "Where else?"

The five friends linked arms and, dipping their heads down against the whirling snow, started to cross the slushy road. Just as they were stepping off the curb, a bloodcurdling howl split the air.

"Ba-*roo!*"

All five girls sprang back onto the sidewalk in alarm. At the same moment, a delivery truck roared by, splattering mud all over them.

"Wow, that was close!" Gwen said, wiping a streak

of dirt from off her face with her mitten. "We could have been flattened by that truck."

"What *was* that noise, anyway?" McGee asked, looking around.

"I think I know." Zan grinned as she pointed back at the bus stop. Sitting beside the green bench was a dog wearing a pink scarf and kitty earmuffs.

"Oscar!" Mary Bubnik cried. "He saved our lives!"

Chapter Four

Hi Lo's tiny restaurant was wedged between a jewelry store and a loan office across the street from the dance studio. A red-and-white sign hanging above the glass door proclaimed, Hi Lo's Pizza and Chinese Food To Go.

"This is the place, Oscar," Mary Bubnik said as she patted the dog on the head. "Wait here, and we'll see if you can come inside."

Gwen was the first to enter the restaurant. As she threw open the glass door, a little brass bell overhead signaled their arrival.

"Hi, Hi!" she shouted, hopping up onto one of the worn red leather stools that ringed the lunch counter.

"We're cold, and we need something warm to drink!"

An elderly Chinese man stuck his head through the small serving window from the kitchen. At the sight of the gang, his lined face creased into a broad smile of welcome.

"Greetings and salutations! What a sunny surprise on such a dreary day. I'll be out in a minute." Hi ducked his head back inside, and a loud clang of pots and pans rang out from the kitchen.

While the others joined Gwen on the stools at the counter, Mary called through the kitchen window, "Hi, we have a new friend we'd like you to meet."

"It would be my pleasure," his voice replied.

"Is it all right if I bring him inside?" Mary asked.

"A him?" Hi's face appeared at the window once more, grinning more than ever. "This *is* a surprise. Tell him to come on in."

"Great! I'll go get him." Mary skipped over to the glass door and held it open. "It's okay, Oscar, you can come in now."

The basset hound stuck his great head through the door and lifted his big black nose in the air. After several curious sniffs, he trotted into the restaurant. The girls watched in amazement as the long dog scurried around the little room, poking his nose into every nook and cranny.

"Wow!" McGee exclaimed. "I didn't think he could move that fast."

"I hope he's housebroken," Gwen muttered under her breath.

"Of course he is," Mary said indignantly. "Oscar is a perfect gentleman. Aren't you, boy?"

The hound, who was busily inhaling a row of crumbs scattered on the floor beneath the booth in the back of the restaurant, looked up. He wagged his tail back and forth, then went back to his work of cleaning the floor of bits of food.

"That's not a dog," Rocky observed. "That's a Hoover vacuum cleaner." The rest of the girls laughed and Rocky added, "Hey, I like that name. Hoover. I think it really suits him."

"Hoover?" Mary repeated. "But his name is Oscar."

"You don't know that," Zan pointed out logically. "His name could be anything."

"Yes, but he answers to Oscar." To demonstrate, Mary Bubnik knelt by the counter and snapped her fingers. "Come here, Oscar."

Without hesitation, the dog trotted over to her side. Mary scratched him behind one ear and said, "See?"

"Oh, yeah?" Rocky hopped off her stool and moved to the far side of the restaurant by the picture window. "Watch this." She knelt down and clucked her tongue several times. "Come here, Hoover. That's a good boy!"

The dog promptly pulled himself up and hurried to sit in front of Rocky. "Good dog, Hoover."

At that moment, Hi pushed open the swinging door from the kitchen and announced, "Here you go, girls! Hi Lo's Hot Chocolate Surprise." The old man's glasses were steamed up from the hot kitchen, and he blinked as he carried a big silver tray with five steaming mugs resting on it.

"Surprise?" Gwen narrowed her eyes suspiciously. "That means you put something weird in it."

"Hi always puts secret ingredients in things," Mary Bubnik reminded her.

"Yes, but usually only in milk shakes, or on pizzas." Gwen was referring to Hi's famous peanut-butter-chocolate shakes, and *Olé!* pizzas that tasted like tacos. "But what sort of surprise could you put in hot chocolate?" Gwen wrinkled her nose as she imagined chunks of peanut butter or bits of jalapeño pepper floating in her cup.

"Taste it," Hi urged, setting one of the white mugs in front of her. Gwen very gingerly took a sip and swallowed. Then she took a much longer sip, and then an even longer sip.

Finally McGee punched her on the arm and demanded, "Well, what's in it?"

Gwen lifted her head and smiled. A moustache of marshmallow and cocoa ringed her mouth. "Cinnamon. And it's delicious."

Hi bowed his head. "Thank you. It's an old family recipe."

As Zan and Mary tasted their drinks, Hi folded his

hands on the counter and looked up expectantly. "I thought you had a boy you wanted me to meet."

"We do," Rocky called from the coat rack. She pointed down at the mutt sitting at her feet. "Hi, meet Hoover."

Hi's eyes widened into two big circles behind his glasses. Before he could say a word, Mary Bubnik hopped off her stool and said stubbornly, "His name is *not* Hoover, it's Oscar. I saw him first, and I named him."

"But . . . but . . . that's a *dog,*" Hi sputtered.

"Not just any dog," Zan said. "That is a Saint Bernasset."

Hi didn't move a muscle. The old man just stared at the dog in disbelief. "Where did you find him?"

"Actually he found us," Mary Bubnik explained. "In the alley next to the ballet academy."

"Yeah," Gwen grumbled, "he found us — and then he took me for all I was worth. My entire food supply is gone."

"That wasn't really food," Zan said. "Those were just snacks."

"And I think he's still hungry." McGee pointed to the dog, who was still sniffing the air. "Do you have anything that he could eat?"

"Well, I might have something in the back," Hi said. "But once I feed him, he has to go outside."

"But why?" Mary asked. "It's so cold out there."

"I'm sorry," Hi said gently. "But dogs aren't allowed in restaurants. That's the law."

"That's a dumb law," Mary said as Hi disappeared back into the kitchen. She knelt down beside the dog and hugged him protectively. "You guys, what are we going to do about Oscar?" Mary glanced over at Rocky and added, "Oscar Hoover."

Zan rubbed her chin thoughtfully. "I wish I could take him to my house, but my mother is very allergic to animals. The only kind of pet I've ever had was a turtle, and he died two days after I got him."

"The same thing happened to my turtle," McGee said. "His shell got all strange and mushy."

"That is totally gross," Gwen said. "It's almost making me lose my appetite." She scooped up one of the marshmallows that was floating in her hot chocolate and repeated, "Almost."

"I've always wanted a dog," Rocky said quietly from the corner. Oscar Hoover had rolled onto his back and one leg was kicking the air as Rocky scratched his belly.

"Me, too," Mary Bubnik said. "My dad never liked them so we never could have one."

"Rocky!" Gwen called as she set her empty cup down on the Formica countertop. "Your hot chocolate is getting cold."

"I'm not really very thirsty," Rocky said. "But I bet Oscar Hoover is. You want my chocolate, boy?"

In answer, the dog rolled to a sitting position and barked one loud woof.

Rocky leaped to her feet in amazement. "He can talk!"

" 'Woof'?" Gwen repeated. "You call that talking?"

"Sure. I asked him a question, and he answered it. Is it his fault that I don't speak dog?"

Rocky grabbed her mug from the counter and set it on the floor in front of the dog. Oscar Hoover delicately licked the marshmallows off the top.

Gwen shook her head. "I can't believe you gave your drink to a dumb dog."

There was a loud clunk as Oscar Hoover knocked the mug on its side. The warm brown liquid streamed out across the linoleum floor.

"Now he's making a total mess," Gwen complained.

"No, he's not," Mary Bubnik retorted. "He's cleaning up the mess."

The dog was following the little river of chocolate with his tongue, lapping it up.

Hi reappeared with his silver tray. This time it held a big white bone sitting on a lace doily. "Here we go — a big bone for a big appetite."

"That bone's as big as Oscar Hoover," Zan said. "What is it?"

Hi placed one of his paper placemats decorated with a big red dragon on the floor and set the bone on top of it. "This is called a T-bone."

At the word T-bone, the dog stopped licking the side of the mug and cocked his head alertly.

"Hey, did you guys see that?" McGee said. "Hi, say that again."

Hi faced the dog and repeated slowly, "T-Bone."

Once again, the dog cocked his head and his ears flapped out to the side.

"Maybe T-Bone is his real name," McGee said, moving to the dog's side. "It fits him perectly."

"But his name is Oscar," Mary Bubnik said stubbornly.

Rocky took her position in the circle around the dog. "His name is Hoover. Look at him inhale that bone."

McGee folded her arms firmly. "I like T-Bone, and that's what I'm going to call him."

"Oscar!" Mary insisted.

"Hoover," Rocky growled.

"T-Bone!" McGee shouted.

Gwen and Zan sided with Mary Bubnik, and soon all five girls were yelling the names at each other, their faces growing redder by the second. All the while, the funny-looking dog chewed contentedly on his bone at their feet, completely oblivious to the argument happening above his head.

Finally Hi covered his ears and bellowed, "Be *quiet!*"

That shut them up fast. None of the girls had ever heard Hi raise his voice before. They looked at him in startled surprise. Hi took off his glasses and polished them on his apron.

"I don't think any of those names fit this dog," he said calmly.

"Well, what would *you* call him?" Gwen asked.

"Einstein," Hi declared, slipping the glasses back onto his nose.

"After the scientist? Why?" Rocky asked.

"Because Einstein was a very smart man." Hi gestured at the dog with his thumb. "This is a very smart mutt. In less than fifteen minutes he has managed to get me to give him my best soup bone, and Rocky to give up a perfectly good cup of hot chocolate. Unfortunately, this same smart dog has made all of you give up a solid friendship and start shouting at each other."

Their eyes all widened in surprise. "We would *never* give up our friendship," Mary exclaimed. "It's too special."

"And we weren't shouting," Rocky insisted. "We were just having a . . . a loud discussion."

"Besides, we have a good excuse," Gwen added. "We've had some terrible news today, and our nerves are on edge."

"What kind of news?" Hi asked.

"Truly the worst kind," Zan replied. "Rocky has to move."

"Move?" Hi repeated. "When?"

"Maybe within the month," Rocky said. "That's

how it's always been before. We're being transferred, and we have to leave immediately."

"This *is* terrible news." Hi slumped down on one of the stools, a stunned look on his face. "I'm so sorry to hear it."

A soft whimper was heard from around their ankles. The girls looked down at the dog and Mary gasped, "Look, Rocky, Oscar is giving you a present to make you feel better."

The dog had carefully placed his bone on Rocky's foot. She knelt down and patted him on the head. "Thank you, boy. I wish I could keep you, Oscar Hoover T-Bone Einstein, but my family's moving."

Mary's face suddenly lit up. "Hey, I just remembered something!"

"What?" Zan asked.

"My parents are divorced."

"You forgot about something as important as that?" Gwen asked in amazement.

"No, silly," Mary said with a giggle. "But my mom loves dogs, and since my dad doesn't live with us anymore, I can probably keep him." Mary wrapped her arms around the basset hound's neck. "Oscar Hoover T-Bone Einstein — you're coming home with me."

"Don't you think you'd better call your mom first?" McGee cautioned her. "And ask her if it's okay?"

"Why should I ask?" Mary replied. "I know she'll say yes!"

Chapter Five

Fifteen minutes later, Mary Bubnik's mother pulled their old green Volvo up to the curb in front of Hi Lo's and tapped the horn three times. The croaking sound that came out sounded more like a frog than a horn.

"I've got to get that fixed," Mrs. Bubnik muttered, adding the horn to her list of fifty other things wrong with the car. She was just about to get out of the car when the door to Hi Lo's restaurant flew open and her daughter appeared.

Mary backed up to the car holding an egg roll in front of Oscar Hoover T-Bone Einstein's nose. Mrs. Bubnik didn't notice her daughter's new companion. She was too busy pushing on the passenger door.

It had a large dent in the side and a tendency to stick, especially in cold weather.

"Pull hard, honey," Mrs. Bubnik called as she beat at the door from the inside.

Mary braced her foot against the side of the car and tugged. The door wrenched open, and Mary fell down hard on the icy sidewalk. But she didn't mind. In fact, Mary was grinning from ear to ear as she stuck her head inside the car and declared, "Mom, I'm bringing Oscar home with me. You're just going to love him. He's smart and lovable — and house-broken, too. I'm sure he won't be any trouble at all."

"Fine, honey," Mrs. Bubnik murmured without really hearing her daughter. She was too busy examining the door handle that had come off in her hand. The knob had long since disappeared, and now it was just a hunk of metal with peeling chrome on the sides.

"You just sit right here, Oscar," Mary said, opening the back door and helping the dog onto the back-seat. "We'll be home in a few minutes." Mary gave him a quick pat, then hopped into the front seat and slammed the door shut by pulling on the torn arm-rest.

"I swear, this car is disintegrating before my very eyes," Mrs. Bubnik grumbled as she tossed the handle in the glove compartment. "Someday it'll just stop, and we'll have to leave it there."

"Don't say things like that," Mary cried protectively. "Mr. Toad is a wonderful car!" She patted the dashboard, and the glove compartment door popped back open.

Without looking Mrs. Bubnik slammed it shut and muttered, "Really wonderful." She slipped the car in gear and the old green Volvo rattled back onto the road. Mrs. Bubnik ran one hand through her hair and turned to smile brightly at her daughter. "So. How was class today?"

"Well . . ." Mary cocked her head to one side. "It was good, and it was bad."

"Tell me the good part first," Mrs. Bubnik said, flicking on the turn signal.

"The Academy is having a big extravaganza ice parade, and I'm going to be in it."

"That *is* good news. When's this supposed to happen?"

"Next Saturday." As Mary talked, she draped one arm between the seats and lazily scratched Oscar under the chin. He laid his huge head on her hand and closed his eyes contentedly. "And there isn't any rehearsal. Basically, we decorate a sled and then skate or ride across the ice in costume. Then the Academy will do a ballet on a stage set up at the end of the lake."

Mrs. Bubnik flicked on the turn signal and guided the car onto Elm Street, the broad, tree-lined boulevard leading up to their apartment complex. "What's the bad news?"

The smile on Mary's face faded. "Rocky has to move. Her dad is being transferred."

Mrs. Bubnik frowned sympathetically. "Oh, I'm sorry to hear that, honey."

Mary shook her head sadly. "The gang just won't be the same without Rocky."

"I know how close y'all are," her mother said, patting Mary on the knee.

"Rocky's parents said she could have a slumber party on Sunday night since there's no school on Monday."

"Good. You girls should have a lot of fun."

"I hope so." Mary leaned her head back against the seat and watched the trunks of the tall elms pass by the car window. The trees were luxurious with leaves in the summertime, but during the winter they just looked like dreary brown skeletons. "I'm sure going to miss Rocky," she said with a sigh.

"I know you will. So will I." Mrs. Bubnik reached for the metal spike where the radio knob used to be and flicked it to the right. "Let's listen to some music. Maybe that'll cheer us up."

Static came out of the speakers, and Mary hit the top of the radio with the heel of her hand. Suddenly the air was filled with the plaintive sound of a country-western singer. When the singer got to the chorus, another lower, more mournful, voice joined him. It began as a low moan, but by the middle of the verse it had turned into a full-fledged, "Ba-*roooo!*"

Mrs. Bubnik froze with her hands gripping the steering wheel as she tried to determine where the eerie sound was coming from. Then she looked in her rearview mirror and almost fainted.

Filling the entire mirror, and only inches from the back of her head, was the face of a hideous furry monster. The beast's head was tilted back, revealing a pair of big slobbering lips and two rows of yellow pointy teeth.

"Mary!" Mrs. Bubnik screamed. "Brace yourself!"

Before Mary knew what was happening, her mother wrenched the car first to the left and then quickly to the right, swerving up over the curb onto the sidewalk. The car came screeching to a halt in front of one of the big elms. Mrs. Bubnik didn't even bother to turn off the engine. Flinging open her door, she unhooked Mary's seat belt and dragged the startled girl across the seat out onto the street.

Meanwhile, the abrupt stop caught Oscar Hoover T-Bone Einstein completely off guard. The dog fell off the seat onto the floor of the car with a thud and a yelp.

"Mom!" Mary gasped. "What's the matter?"

"Some *thing* is in the backseat," Mrs. Bubnik whispered hoarsely as she inched up to the sputtering car.

Mary tapped her mother on the shoulder. "Mom, that thing is Oscar."

"Oscar?"

"Well, his full name is Oscar Hoover T-Bone Einstein, but I like Oscar best. He's named after Dad's brother."

"Mary!" Mrs. Bubnik exclaimed, spinning around to face her daughter. "What in blue blazes are you talking about?"

"Him."

Mary pointed at the open car door just as Oscar, who had managed to squeeze into the front seat, hopped out of the car. As he did, the car lurched forward into the trunk of the big elm tree and died.

"A dog?" Mrs. Bubnik cried exasperatedly. "I don't believe it!"

"Isn't he wonderful?" Mary cooed, hugging Oscar around the neck.

"Mary, you know we can't keep him," her mother said.

"Why can't we?" Mary cried. "I promise I'll take care of him. You won't have to do a thing."

"Mary, look at him. He nearly scared me to death. And he'd probably eat us out of house and home."

"I'll work after school to pay for him. Really."

"It's out of the question," her mother said flatly. "The vet bills alone would break our budget."

"Please!" Mary wailed. "He won't get sick. I promise."

Mrs. Bubnik stared hard at her daughter and the funny-looking dog that sat calmly beside her. Finally, she sighed and said, "Put him in the car, and I'll think about it on the way home."

Moments later they were back in Mr. Toad, heading for home. A passerby had helped Mrs. Bubnik roll the car back onto the street and get it started again.

They rode along in silence, with the dog sitting in the back, resting his head across the seat on Mary's shoulder. Every now and then Mary heaved a loud sigh, but her mother said nothing.

The Bubniks' apartment complex consisted of four boxy buildings clustered around a grassy courtyard, with a pool shaped like a jelly bean in the center. Mrs. Bubnik parked the Volvo in the parking lot, and then Mary and the dog followed her up the concrete steps to their apartment door. Once inside the apartment, Mrs. Bubnik turned to her daughter and said, "I'll let you keep him on a trial basis."

Mary jumped up and down and shrieked, "Yea! Mom, you're the greatest — "

"And on one condition," Mrs. Bubnik said, raising a finger. "That you give him a bath right away." She looked at the dog and wrinkled her nose. "He stinks to high heaven."

"Oh, a bath's fine with you, isn't it, Oscar?" Mary cried. At the mention of the word "bath," the dog's ears flattened against his head and his eyes narrowed into little red slits, but Mary ignored the warning. "We'll do it right now." She skipped to the bathroom and turned on the taps in the tub.

"Mary, make sure you use those ratty old towels in the back of the linen closet," Mrs. Bubnik called, as she poured herself a glass of cola and took it into the living room.

"Okay, Mom!" While Mary bustled around the bathroom, stacking towels on the toilet seat and a fresh bar of soap and a bottle of shampoo on the edge of the tub, the basset hovered just outside the door, staring at her suspiciously. Finally Mary knelt down on the tiled floor and, patting her knee, called, "Come on, Oscar. It's bath time."

He promptly tucked his tail between his legs and made a beeline for the living room.

"*Oscar!*" Mary raced after him, chasing him around the room twice. The dog tried to squeeze under the coffee table to hide. Unfortunately, he was too big and it flipped over, spilling Mrs. Bubnik's glass full of soda all over the carpet.

"Get a sponge, quick!" Mrs. Bubnik called, frantically trying to get her magazines and books out of the way of the dripping liquid.

Mary grabbed a sponge from the sink and tossed it to her mother, then dove for the dog, who was scurrying down the hall. She caught him by the leg just as he was slipping under the bed in the back bedroom.

"Oh, no, you don't!" Mary said, dragging him back down the hallway. "You're not getting away from me that easily."

Mary wrestled him into the bathroom and shut the door. Then she groaned as she hoisted him over the edge of the bathtub. "Boy, you're heavy."

When Oscar hit the water, he let out a wail that sounded like the noon whistle that went off every day at the fire station.

"Oh, stop that, Oscar," Mary said, as she poured a thick line of shampoo down his back. "It'll all be over in a minute." She rubbed his back and as big handfuls of suds oozed out of his matted fur, Oscar howled even louder.

"Now don't be a baby," Mary said, soaping his head.

"Mary, can't you get him to stop that?" Mrs. Bubnik called from the living room. "The neighbors are going to complain." The doorbell rang right on cue and Mrs. Bubnik said, "See? I told you." She peeked through the peephole, made a sour face, and whispered, "It's that grumpy Mrs. Stubbson from next door. I knew it."

"Don't let her in!" Mary pleaded. "Oscar will be good. I just won't give him a bath at home anymore."

"Rosie Bubnik?" the old lady called from outside. "Have you got a dog in there?"

Mrs. Bubnik cracked the door open an inch. "Why?"

"Because it's against the rules."

"What do you mean? You've got a cat."

"You know very well that cats are allowed," the

old woman retorted, pushing her way into the apartment. "But dogs smell and make messes on the grass." The dog let out another howl and Mrs. Stubbson added, "Plus, they make too much noise."

"I'm sure the rules can be bent a little bit," Mrs. Bubnik said. "We just brought the dog home and he's taking a little time to get adjusted."

"He'll just have to get unadjusted. If the other tenants don't want a dog, then you can't have him."

Mary listened anxiously to their conversation as she tried to rinse the shampoo out of Oscar's fur.

"I'll talk to the neighbors tomorrow," Mrs. Bubnik said, "and see if they think it's all right."

"You're talking to one neighbor right now," Mrs. Stubbson replied, "and I say *no*."

Mary couldn't stand it anymore. She left the dog in the bathtub and marched out into the hall with soap and water still dripping from her hands.

"Mrs. Stubbson, how can you be so mean?" Mary cried indignantly. "Your cat is fat and grumpy, he cries at everyone's door, tears up the plants by the pool, and gets into the garbage, but we don't complain."

"Mary, please." Mrs. Bubnik wrapped her arm around her daughter. "Don't shout at Mrs. Stubbson."

"Yes, young lady," Mrs. Stubbson huffed. "Mind your manners."

"You mind yours," Mary snapped back. "We didn't

invite you over. You barged in — just like your cat."

Mrs. Stubbson's mouth opened and shut like a fish. "How dare you!"

"Hey, what's going on in there?" a man's voice called from outside the open door. "Mrs. Stubbson, are you all right?"

A triumphant smile spread across Mrs. Stubbson's face. "That's Mr. Martinez, the manager. He'll be *very* interested to know what you have in there."

"Please, Mrs. Stubbson," Mary's mother pleaded softly, "let me tell him in my own way."

A loud thud sounded from the bathroom and Oscar burst into the living room, covered from head to toe in soapsuds. With his feet slipping and sliding, he headed straight for Mrs. Stubbson.

"Keep that beast away from me," she screamed, backing away in fright.

The dog, in a mighty leap for the door, knocked Mrs. Stubbson into the apartment manager, who was standing on the outside landing. The two adults crashed into the railing, knocking a big ceramic planter onto the ground below. It crashed against the sidewalk and broke into a thousand pieces.

There was a deathly silence as Mr. Martinez and Mrs. Stubbson glared at the dog, who was calmly licking soapsuds off his front paws.

"I guess Oscar can't stay with us," Mary finally said in a tiny voice.

"No, honey," Mrs. Bubnik said sadly. "He can't."

Chapter Six

The next morning the Hays's phone rang just as Gwen was shuffling into the kitchen.

"I'll get it!" she shouted to the house in general. Gwen didn't receive that many phone calls, but she wanted to be the first to know about it when she did. Gwen picked up the receiver and declared, "Hays Sanitarium. Which nut do you want to talk to?"

There was a long pause. Then a voice said, "Gwen, it's me, Mary. I'm in trouble."

Gwen hurried to the cookie jar for a handful of chocolate chip cookies and settled onto the high wooden stool by the kitchen counter. "What's wrong?"

"It's Oscar."

"Who?"

"Oscar Hoover T-Bone Einstein," Mary explained.

"Oh, that dog." Gwen bit off a large chunk of cookie and mumbled, "What's happened to him?"

"Nothing," Mary replied. "But something's going to happen to me if I don't get rid of him right away."

"Well, just put him outside your front door, and shut it."

"Gwen!" Mary gasped. "That's an *awful* thing to say. It's cold out there, and he'd be scared."

"Well, what do you want *me* to do about it?"

"Take him."

Gwen took another large bite of cookie. "Take him where?"

"To your house."

"No way!" Gwen shouted, spraying crumbs all over the counter. "My mom would never go for it. She can't stand anything that drools or sheds. And he does both."

"Well, what else can I do?" Mary cried. "He can't stay here."

"Try McGee," Gwen suggested. "She lives on that farm in Fairview. That'd be the perfect place."

"I tried calling her, but no one was home."

Gwen had crammed another cookie into her mouth. It made her cheeks puff up like a chipmunk, and her words came out funny when she tried to speak. "Hab ooh twied Wan?"

"Zan can't help," Mary replied. "Remember? Her

mother is allergic to animal hair." Mary lowered her voice to an urgent whisper. "Gwen, *please!* Just take him till Monday. I need time to find him a home. Oscar stayed here last night, and the apartment manager got so upset he threatened to evict us. Please. It's a matter of life and death!"

Little bits of chocolate chip skittered across the countertop as Gwen said, "I just know my mom won't like it."

"Well, go and ask her if it's okay."

"I can't. She's at the store, getting supplies for me to take to the slumber party tonight."

"Slumber party?" Mary gasped. "I forgot all about it!"

"How could you forget?" Gwen asked. "It may be the last party the five us will ever have."

"Make that four," Mary said in her most pitiful voice. "I can't go. I've got to find Oscar a home."

Gwen swallowed her cookie with a gulp. "Okay, okay! You can bring that dog here. But only for *one* night."

"Oh, thank you, Gwen," Mary gushed. "I'll be eternally grateful."

"You better be," Gwen joked. Just before she hung up, she added, "Bring your pj's when you bring the mutt. Then my mom can drive us to Rocky's."

An hour later Gwen was sitting on her front porch, still munching on a cookie, when the Bubniks' old green Volvo turned into her driveway. The rear passenger door swung open and Mary hopped out, her corduroy backpack shaped like a bear slung over her shoulder. Lumbering right behind her was Oscar Hoover T-Bone Einstein — wearing sunglasses. He sat patiently beside Mary as she said good-bye to her mother.

"I forgot how ugly he was," Gwen said as she watched the sausage-shaped dog plod up the drive. "Is that why he's wearing sunglasses? As a disguise?"

"The sun hurts his eyes. And don't call him ugly." Mary Bubnik leaned over and patted him on the head. "Well, Oscar, this is your new home. What do you think?"

The dog replied by carefully removing the rest of Gwen's cookie from her hand and swallowing it whole.

"Hey, you thief, that was mine!" Gwen scolded as he prodded her hand with his wet nose, searching for another cookie. "Yuck!" Gwen grimaced and hurriedly wiped her hand on her blouse. "And this is *not* your home. I want you to think of it more as a motel, where you'll be staying for *one* night, and one night only."

At the scolding sound of Gwen's voice, the dog's ears drooped and he hung his head, peering mournfully over the top of his sunglasses at her.

"Hey!" a voice shouted from the street in front of the house. Gwen and Mary turned to see a blond-haired boy on an electric blue mountain bike, popping wheelies as he weaved figure eights. "Hey, you!" he shouted again.

Gwen clutched Mary Bubnik's arm and hissed, "It's him! Eddie O'Rourke, the Hunk! I have lived on this street for three years and he has never, *ever*, spoken a single word to me."

"Well, you'd better answer him, or he may never speak to you again," Mary said with a giggle.

"Were you by any chance talking to me?" Gwen called, pointing to herself with her finger. Immediately she muttered under her breath, "I can't believe I said that. He's going to think I'm a total idiot."

Eddie ran his bike up onto the sidewalk and skidded to an abrupt halt. He put one foot on the ground, keeping the other perched on the pedal, and leaned his elbows on his handlebars. "Is that your dog?"

"Him?" Gwen leaned as far away as she could from the basset. "Uh, er, um . . ."

Before she could say no, the boy added, "He is one cool dog."

Gwen's hand instantly shot out and she patted Oscar Hoover T-Bone Einstein vigorously on the head. "Yeah, he's my dog. I just got him today."

"How'd you get him to wear the shades?"

Gwen shrugged. "He came with them."

"Cool." The boy slid off his bike and rolled it up the drive toward them.

"He's coming this way!" Gwen whispered to Mary out of the corner of her mouth. "What should I do?"

Mary, who was never shy about meeting anyone, shrugged pleasantly. "Keep talking."

Eddie leaned his bike against the side of the house and knelt down beside the dog. "Is he friendly?"

"Uh, yes," Gwen replied. "I think."

"He's very friendly," Mary jumped in. "He loves people — especially boys." Mary wiggled her eyebrows for emphasis and giggled. Gwen jabbed her in the ribs with an elbow and Mary yelped, "Ouch! Why'd you do that?"

Gwen shot Mary her best "If-you-say-another-word-I'll-murder-you" look, and then smiled back at Eddie. "Go ahead and pet him."

Eddie held his hand out palm up and said, "Hiya, boy. Give me five."

To their surprise, Oscar Hoover T-Bone Einstein raised his front paw and slapped it against the boy's palm.

Eddie laughed. "This is the coolest dog I have ever seen. What's his name?"

"His name?" Gwen repeated. All of the names everyone had given the dog rattled through her brain and she couldn't decide which one to use. "Um, actually, he doesn't have an official one yet." She added coyly, "What do you think I should call him?"

Eddie scratched the dog behind one floppy ear. "Well, with his sunglasses and totally laid-back attitude, this dog's pretty slick. That's what I'd call him. Slick."

"Slick." Mary tried the name out thoughtfully. She didn't like it much, but she didn't want to let on and maybe ruin things for Gwen. "That's . . . that's a nice name."

"Nice?" Gwen rolled her eyes at her friend. "Mary, Slick is a very cool name."

As if in answer, Oscar Hoover T-Bone Einstein Slick yawned broadly and laid his head in Gwen's lap.

"Look, Gwen!" Mary squealed. "He really likes you."

"Well, of course, he likes me," Gwen replied, as a pleasant warmth covered her face. She hugged the dog's big head and said, "He's my dog, isn't he?"

"Boy, are you lucky," Eddie said wistfully. "My parents won't let me have any kind of pet."

Gwen hugged the dog again. "Any time you want to visit Slick, just stop over."

"All *right*." The boy grinned happily at Gwen as he swung onto his bike. "So long, Slick!"

Oscar Hoover T-Bone Einstein Slick lifted his head and let out a warm woof of farewell.

"Outstanding!" Eddie crowed, bouncing his bike off the sidewalk onto the street. "I'll catch you later," he called back over his shoulder as he rode off.

Gwen waited until Eddie was out of hearing range, and then she leaped to her feet and squealed, "Did you hear that? Eddie O'Rourke just told me, Gwendolyn Hays, that he would catch me later!"

"So?"

"So that means that he's going to come by and visit again." Gwen hopped up and down in a little jig of celebration. Then she put her hands on her hips and declared, "Boy, won't that make the Neergards jealous!"

"Who are the Neergards?" Mary Bubnik asked.

"Just the most popular girls at my school." Gwen gestured with her thumb over her shoulder. "They live right across the street and totally ignore me. I mean, the three of us wait at the bus stop together every morning, but they act like I'm invisible." Gwen leaned down and patted the dog on the head. "Well, O'Rourke is going to change all that."

"O'Rourke?" Mary tilted her head in confusion. "I thought his name was Slick."

"Oh, I just let Eddie call him that because I couldn't think of a better name at the moment."

"I thought Oscar was a good name — " Mary began, but Gwen cut her off.

"It was a fine name when he was your dog, but he's mine now, so *I* get to name him. And I'm naming him after Eddie O'Rourke." She hugged the dog so hard his sunglasses fell off. "Eddie O'Rourke Hays. That sounds great."

"But what about when Eddie comes to visit?" Mary asked.

"Then he can be Slick," Gwen said simply. She

scratched the dog beneath the chin. "You don't mind, do you, boy?"

He thumped the ground twice with his heavy tail. Gwen leaped to her feet, shouting, "Eddie O'Rourke is coming to visit *me*." She stuck her tongue out at the house across the street. "Take that, *Sneergards*!"

Mary giggled right along with her friend. "I guess this means you've changed your mind about Oscar — I mean, O'Rourke — staying here only one night."

"Are you kidding?" Gwen flung her arms out wide and twirled about in a circle. "Eddie O'Rourke can stay here for the rest of his life!"

"Good," Mary said. "Now tell your mom that."

"Mom." Gwen instantly stopped spinning. "What do you mean?"

Mary pointed to the big white Cadillac slowing down to turn into the driveway. "Isn't that her?"

"Yes — oh, no!" Gwen grabbed the dog by the neck and began pulling him onto the porch. "This is terrible. I'm not ready." Gwen kicked open the front door with her foot and shouted, "Quick, get Eddie O'Rourke in the house and stand in front of him."

"Why do you want to hide him?" Mary asked, pushing the dog through the front door.

"You don't know my mother," Gwen explained, as

she watched the hound vanish into the living room. "I mean, you don't just spring something like a dog on her. It takes days of planning. First you mention in an offhand way how much you'd like to have a dog. Then you leave cute dog pictures lying around the house. Then you comment on how a lot of burglaries have been happening to houses in Deerfield that don't have guard dogs. *Then,* when you think she's in a really good mood, you *casually* mention Eddie O'Rourke — "

"Oh, Gwen! There's not enough time for all that." Mary squeezed her friend's hand as they stood side by side on the porch and waited for Mrs. Hays to get out of the car. "But don't worry. I just know that when she sees him, she'll fall instantly in love."

Gwen swallowed hard. "I hope you're right."

"Hello, Mary," Mrs. Hays called as she stepped out of her car. "Why don't you girls come help me with the groceries?"

Gwen and Mary didn't move. Behind them they could hear the dog busily exploring the living room.

"Well, come on," Mrs. Hays said, pulling a bag out of the trunk. "What are you waiting for?"

"We, um, er, have a — a surprise for you," Gwen stammered.

"Oh, really?" Mrs. Hays smiled prettily. In her crisply tailored green skirt-and-jacket ensemble, with matching pumps and scarf, Gwen's mother cut a striking figure. She was one of those women who was always stylishly dressed, no matter what the occasion. That made her the complete opposite of Gwen. "I like surprises," Mrs. Hays said, stepping onto the porch. "What is it?"

The two girls stepped apart and sang out, "Ta-da!"

The hound was sitting just inside the door, grinning at them. Gwen gasped as she recognized the antique pillow Mrs. Hays had bought in England. It was caught on one of his teeth. He had torn it to shreds, and the stuffing was strewn all over the white carpet around him.

"AAAAAAAHHHHHHHHHHHHH!"

Mrs. Hays screamed so loudly that several neighbors came running to their doors. She dropped her bag of groceries on the porch and a large bottle of diet cola exploded, splattering liquid everywhere. Gwen's mother charged past the two girls, shouting, "Give me that, you disgusting creature!"

Mary turned to Gwen and said, "I guess this means you can't keep him, huh?"

Gwen blinked behind her glasses. "You guessed right."

Chapter Seven

That evening Gwen and Mary Bubnik stood on the Garcias' front porch, clutching a piece of clothesline that was wrapped around Oscar Hoover T-Bone Einstein Slick Eddie O'Rourke's neck.

"I still think we should have called Rocky, and asked her if it was okay to bring Oscar — I mean, O'Rourke," Mary said nervously.

Gwen shook her head. "This way's much better — we have the element of surprise working for us."

"We had that working for us with your mother, and she nearly had a hissy fit," Mary Bubnik reminded her. "Is she always that jumpy?"

"Only when she's watching her favorite antique

be systematically destroyed by a weird, overgrown mutt."

Mary Bubnik asked nervously, "What if Mrs. Garcia says we can't bring him into the party?"

Gwen shrugged. "Then we'll keep him outside."

The two girls were still standing on the porch, trying to get up their nerve to ring the doorbell, when a blue sedan with police flashers on its roof screeched to a halt in the driveway.

"Uh-oh," Mary groaned. "It's Rocky's dad."

Sergeant Garcia leaped out of the patrol car and came up the sidewalk at a run, without even bothering to shut the door. The sound of voices exchanging clipped messages on the car's CB crackled through the air.

"And he's in a hurry," Gwen muttered.

"Get in the house, girls!" the sergeant ordered, taking the porch steps two at a time. The shiny silver badge on his black beret flashed in the darkness. "It isn't safe out here."

Gwen and Mary looked at each other uncertainly.

"Move!"

When Rocky's dad barked an order, people obeyed. Gwen shoved open the front door and the girls rushed inside, dragging the hound behind.

"Anita! Kids!" Sergeant Garcia bellowed, rushing past the girls into the house. "Everybody in the den, on the double!"

Rocky's brother Michael appeared in the doorway of the kitchen, chewing on a slice of pizza. David and Joey charged out of their bedroom, slapping each other with bath towels. Jay, who was the oldest and already in college, was on his back under the dining room table, fixing a wobbly leg. He slid out onto the rug, clutching a screwdriver, and asked, "What's up?"

"Family meeting," Sergeant Garcia replied as he quickly dialed their telephone. "Pronto."

Gwen and Mary hustled the dog down the hall into the den, where Rocky, Zan, and McGee were already sitting by the TV, drinking Cokes. They looked up at Mary and Gwen, who were standing in the door, white-faced and speechless.

"You guys look awful," Rocky cried out in alarm. "What happened?"

Mary's mouth opened and closed as she gestured back over her shoulder down the hall.

"Did my brothers do something to you?" Rocky demanded. "I'll get them." She threw her head back and screamed, *"Mo-ther!* The boys are at it again."

In the meantime, Zan and McGee clustered around the dog, hugging him and cooing in his ears.

"What's he doing here?" McGee asked. "I thought you were going to take him, Mary."

Mary swallowed hard and then said carefully, "I was, and then Gwen was. Zan couldn't, and you weren't home. . . ." She looked at Rocky hopefully. "So Rocky gets him."

"*Mo—!*" Rocky stopped in mid-scream. "I get him? No way. We're moving."

"Sorry," Gwen said, "but you have to take him. At least for tonight."

"Has my mother seen him yet?" Rocky asked worriedly.

Before anyone could answer, Sergeant Garcia led the rest of the Garcia clan into the den. The girls all jumped in front of the dog, shielding him from view. The three youngest boys flopped onto the sofa, while Jay turned off the TV. Rocky's father waited until Mrs. Garcia had come in, then strode to the center of the room.

"All right, everyone, listen up," Sergeant Garcia said. "Late this afternoon, a prisoner escaped from lockup and— "

"A convict's on the loose?" Joey asked. "Cool."

Sergeant Garcia gave him a stern look and continued. "He was last spotted around eighteen hundred hours entering the base housing compound."

"The guy's in our neighborhood?" Rocky asked, wide-eyed.

"We have reason to think so." Her father widened his stance slightly, clasping his hands behind his back. "Every man on the security force is searching the area. But until we find him, it is imperative that all personnel stay confined to quarters."

"But Dad, I was going to meet my buddies at the teen club," Michael protested.

"The teen club is closed for tonight," his father responded. "The base is on full alert."

"This sounds really scary," Mary Bubnik said in a tiny voice.

"Don't worry, we'll get him." Sergeant Garcia smiled at her warmly. "You will all be fine if you just follow orders, and stay inside."

Mrs. Garcia put her hand on her husband's shoulder. "Maybe we should call their mothers and have them take the girls home."

"No can do," Sergeant Garcia replied. "The base is cordoned off. No one gets in or out without special orders from the base commander."

"We're trapped!" Gwen gasped. "What if we run out of food?"

McGee nudged her hard with an elbow. "Get real, Hays."

Sergeant Garcia moved to the sliding glass doors opening onto the patio. He clicked the lock and drew the shades. "In the meantime, I want all windows and doors locked, curtains drawn, and no one — I mean, *no one* — leaves the premises. That's an order."

"Yes, sir," the Garcia kids snapped in unison.

Sergeant Garcia turned to his oldest son, Jay, and said, "Help out your mother, you hear? I'm leaving you in charge of your younger brothers and sister and her friends."

"Yes, sir."

"If anything happens, call the station. They'll catch up with me wherever I am." He adjusted his beret, kissed Mrs. Garcia on the cheek, and headed for the door.

"Wait a minute!" Gwen sang out, stopping him in the door. "What if the convict comes to the house, cuts the phone lines, and holds us hostage?"

Sergeant Garcia chuckled. "That won't happen, I promise you." As he turned to leave, Rocky's dad nearly tripped over Oscar Hoover T-Bone Einstein Slick Eddie O'Rourke, who'd slipped out from behind the girls. Sergeant Garcia looked up in shock. "What is *this?*"

"That's our dog, Dad," Rocky explained quickly. "Remember, you said if we moved, we could get one? Well, we're moving, so I got one."

"But . . . but I meant *after* we moved," her father sputtered in confusion.

Rocky threw her arms around her father desperately. "Oh, can I keep him, Dad, please?"

Her father frowned. "We'll deal with it later." He turned to his wife and said, "I'll call as soon as we hear anything." Then he was out the door. Moments later they heard the patrol car roar off into the night.

"Whew!" Rocky said, scratching the dog behind the ear. "That was a close one."

"Not so fast, young lady," Mrs. Garcia said. "That dog goes outside."

"But, Mom, Dad said— "

"We'll deal with it later, I know. Until later gets here, that dog goes straight into the backyard."

"But there's a convict on the loose," Rocky wailed. "He could get hurt."

Mrs. Garcia folded her arms across her chest. "Out. That's an order." She turned to her sons and said, "Boys, come help me lock up the house."

The boys leaped to their feet and followed her out of the den.

"Wow, your mom's as strict as your dad," Mary Bubnik said. "She should have been in the Air Force."

"How do you think they met?" Rocky retorted. She grabbed the dog by the collar and tugged him toward the sliding-glass door. "Come on, Hoover. You'll have to take your chances outside."

The dog dug in his heels and refused to budge.

"One of you guys give me a hand," Rocky said.

McGee got behind him and shoved hard, but the dog dropped his shoulders close to the ground and sat there like a lump.

"Geez Louise, he's strong," McGee gasped. "You all have to help."

Gwen, Zan, and Mary Bubnik joined Rocky and McGee and soon all five were straining to budge the reluctant hound. But nothing worked. Beads of sweat streaked their foreheads. Finally Rocky shouted down the hall, "Mom, he really doesn't want to go out. Can't he stay inside?"

"Rocky, I told you to put him out and I meant it," her mom shouted back. "Now do as I say."

Rocky bit her lip. "What're we going to do?"

Gwen straightened up suddenly. "I've got an idea. Where's the food?"

"Gwen, this is no time for a snack," McGee barked. "Can't you give your stomach a break?"

"It isn't for me," Gwen retorted. "It's for Eddie O'Rourke." She turned back to Rocky. "Where are the goodies?"

Rocky pointed to the coffee table, where a couple of pizza boxes had been stacked. "Over there."

"Perfect." Gwen hurried over and flipped open the top box. The smell of cheese and pepperoni filled the room and the dog sat up immediately. He watched Gwen intently as she pulled a slice out of the box. She scooped up a long strand of melted cheese dripping off the side and dropped it into her mouth. "Ummmmm!"

Oscar Hoover T-Bone Einstein Slick Eddie O'Rourke made a beeline right for her. Gwen smiled triumphantly as she picked off a tiny piece of pepperoni and dropped it toward the floor. The hound lunged for it, snapping his jaws shut so hard his teeth rattled.

"Gee, I think I'll just take a walk outside," Gwen said nonchalantly as she moved to the sliding door. The dog followed right at her heels, never taking his eyes off the pizza. McGee unlocked the door, and Gwen opened it just wide enough to toss the slice onto the patio. The dog jammed himself through the narrow opening and hurried to scoop it up. McGee slammed the door shut after him and everyone applauded.

"Way to go!" Rocky exulted.

Mary Bubnik peered anxiously through the curtain onto the patio. "You sure he's going to be all right out there?"

"Sure," Rocky declared. "That prisoner isn't going to mess with an ugly old dog."

"*That* sure made me hungry," Gwen remarked, strolling back to the coffee table. "I think I'll have a slice of my own."

"Don't touch that food!" a voice barked from the door. A figure clad in a black turtleneck and camouflage pants leaped into the room. He had a black ski mask over his face, and Mary Bubnik screamed with fright.

"It's him!" she cried, grabbing Zan by the arm and almost knocking her to the floor. "The escaped prisoner."

"This house is now under martial law," the figure

declared. "Which gives me control over all provisions. Like pizza."

"Like huh!" Rocky put her hands on her hips. "This is *my* food for *my* party."

"Rocky!" Mary whispered nervously. "I don't think it's a good idea to get the terrorist upset."

"What are you talking about?" Rocky retorted. "It's just my wimpy brother dressed up like a commando."

Michael pulled off his ski mask and grinned. "Look, Rocky, Dad left Jay in charge, and he said we could eat anything we wanted."

"Did not." Rocky put herself in front of the food and clenched her fists.

"Did so."

"Did not."

Michael was about to lunge for the table when a bone-chilling wail froze them all in their tracks.

"Wha — what was that?" Michael stammered, licking his lips nervously.

"I never heard anything so awful in my entire life," Zan whispered.

"Do you think it's . . . ?" Mary's voice died away without finishing her sentence, but everyone knew what she was talking about.

Mrs. Garcia burst into the room, followed by Jay, who was holding a hammer in one hand and a crowbar in the other. "What in God's name was that?" she asked.

The sound swelled to a deafening pitch, then it broke into a pathetic bark.

"It's Hoover!" Rocky cried, running to the window and pulling open the curtain. The basset was staring forlornly through the glass into the room.

"He's scared," Zan cried.

"Can't we bring him inside?" Rocky pleaded.

"Rocky, I told you already," Mrs. Garcia replied. "We can't — " The dog let out another painful yowl and Mrs. Garcia covered her ears. "Is he going to keep that up all night?"

"Not if we let him in," McGee said with a sly grin.

Mrs. Garcia stared at the dog for a long moment and shook her head. "Oh, I don't know," she muttered.

Oscar Hoover T-Bone Einstein Slick Eddie O'Rourke stared up at her solemnly. Then he raised one paw and lightly scratched the glass.

"All right, he can sleep in the garage." The girls cheered happily and Mrs. Garcia cut them off with a warning. "But if I hear any more noise out of that dog tonight, I'm calling the Humane Society."

"He'll be good, Mom," Rocky said, as she slid open the door. "I promise."

"Hurry up and close the door," Michael yelled. "That prisoner may be right outside."

The girls screamed as one. Rocky jerked the startled dog into the den and slammed the door shut with a crash.

"Michael, do you have to be so dramatic?" Mrs.

Garcia asked in a tired voice. A creaking sound came from the corner, and they all turned to see the basset struggling to climb up on the recliner.

"Not on your father's favorite chair!" Mrs. Garcia yelled, grabbing a magazine and rolling it up. "Scat, you . . . you — "

Rocky threw herself between her mother and the dog. "It's okay, Mom, I've got the situation under control." Rocky motioned to the gang. "Come on, guys, help me get him into the garage."

Rocky wrapped her arms around his middle, and McGee and Zan picked up each end. Mary cupped his head in her hands, and Gwen carried his tail. They hustled him down the hall, through the kitchen into the garage. Rocky shut the door and breathed a sigh of relief. "There."

"Are you sure he's okay in there?" Zan asked as the dog whimpered softly behind the door.

"He'll need some water, that's for sure," McGee declared.

"Not to mention some food," Gwen added.

Zan grabbed a bucket from the broom closet and filled it with water from the kitchen sink. The others rummaged through Mrs. Garcia's pantry for some food. Within minutes they'd piled candy bars, potato chips, and miscellaneous leftovers in a big mixing bowl and left it with the dog.

"That should hold him for a while," McGee declared as the girls trooped back into the den.

"Did you have to give him those chocolate-covered granola bars, Mary?" Gwen muttered as she hungrily dug into a cold piece of pizza. "That seems really wasted on a dog."

"Why shouldn't he have a special treat?" Mary replied defensively. "Just because he's a dog doesn't mean he has to eat like one."

"Hey, you guys," Rocky said, passing out pillows and sleeping bags to the others. "I had my mom rent this cool movie for us to watch."

"Great," McGee said. "What is it?"

"Bad Dream on Oak Street, Part Twelve."

The others stared at her in dismay. Rocky laughed and said, "Just kidding."

Chapter Eight

"You guys?" McGee's voice called softly out of the darkness a few hours later. They had all spread their sleeping bags on the floor of the den. "Are you awake?"

"I am now," Gwen said, rolling over.

"What about you, Rocky?" McGee asked.

"Mmmph," Rocky rumbled into her pillow.

McGee sat up in her sleeping bag and cocked her head. "I think I heard something. By the window."

"Cut it out, McGee," Mary Bubnik pleaded, squeezing her pillow to her chest. "You're scaring me."

"I'm not kidding," McGee said. "It sounded like a

scraping sound. As if someone were trying to get in."

Gwen groped on the rug for her glasses. For some reason she always heard better with them on. She stared intently through the darkness at the sliding-glass doors. The only sounds in the quiet house were the hum of the refrigerator in the kitchen and one of the Garcia boys snoring down the hall. "Are you sure you heard something?"

"I'm positive. It sounded like a branch scraping across the glass." McGee was out of her sleeping bag and creeping toward the door. Suddenly she froze in place and hissed, "Listen, there it is again."

Zan sat bolt upright. "It couldn't have been a branch."

"How come?" Gwen asked.

"Because the Garcias only have one tree in their backyard," Zan explained, "and it's nowhere near the house." Zan was very observant. She had trained herself to notice details because she hoped to become a private eye some day, like her favorite fictional heroine, Tiffany Truenote.

Scritch — scritch.

"Oooh, you guys," Mary moaned. "I heard it that time." She reached out and shook Rocky's shoulder. "Rocky, get up. Someone's at the sliding-glass doors."

Rocky rolled over and groaned, "Cut it out, you wimps. It's probably just Hoover messing around."

"Oh, thank goodness." Mary fell back against her pillow, but no sooner had her head touched the pillow than she sprang back up again. "But if we put him in the garage, what's he doing in the backyard?"

This time it was Rocky's turn to sit up. She scrambled out of her sleeping bag and headed for the kitchen. "I'll see if Hoover is still in the garage."

"Ouch!" Gwen cried out as Rocky stomped on her leg in the dark. "Watch where you're going."

"Sorry," Rocky mumbled as she picked her way through the cluster of sleeping bags on the rug.

"Don't turn on the light," Zan cautioned. "If someone's at the window, we want to be able to see him."

"I don't want to see him," Mary whimpered, covering her head with her pillow.

Rocky tiptoed across the tiled kitchen floor and slowly opened the door to the garage. "Hoover?" She whistled softly. "Are you there, boy?"

She listened for the click of his nails on the concrete, but there was no sound. Rocky grabbed the flashlight her father kept on a shelf to the right of the door and flicked it on. She flashed the light around the garage, making sure to keep the beam low to the ground. Her mother's blue Dodge van was parked in its slot. A scattered pile of empty candy bars and chewed cardboard lay beside it. But Oscar Hoover T-Bone Einstein Slick Eddie O'Rourke was nowhere to be seen.

"Oh, no," she murmured as the beam hit the

utility door leading into the backyard.

"What?" a voice whispered behind her. Rocky almost leaped out of her skin. Gwen and the others had crept into the kitchen and stood together in a tight little cluster behind Rocky.

"You almost gave me a heart attack," Rocky gasped. "What's the idea sneaking up on me like that, anyway?"

"What did you say 'Oh, no' about?" Zan asked softly.

"Hoover's escaped." Rocky gestured with the flashlight to the utility door. The Garcia boys had piled boxes against it to form a barricade, but the door had been wedged open about six inches.

"He would have really had to suck in his stomach to get through that opening," McGee said, peering at the tiny crack.

"He would have had to suck in his brain," Gwen muttered. "Nothing could get through there."

"Well, he's not here, and that's the only opening," Rocky said.

"We'd better go get him," Mary Bubnik declared, stepping into the garage. She was wearing her pink pajamas with cats printed all over them, and matching pink fuzzy slippers that made little scuffling sounds as she padded across the concrete to the door.

"What do you think you're doing?" Gwen demanded in a loud hiss. She was in her usual sleeping garb — a baggy red sweatshirt over a pair of gray sweatpants.

"I'm going to save Oscar," Mary called back over her shoulder. "There's a convict on the loose."

"Are you out of your mind?" Gwen squeaked from inside the kitchen. "We could get hurt."

"You don't have to come," Mary replied. "Just hold the door for me. I'll go get him."

"I'm not letting you go out there by yourself," Rocky declared. "Besides, I know the territory."

"Geez Louise, you sound like you're going into the jungle or something," McGee said. The huge red-and-white football jersey that she wore as a nightgown hung down to her knees, almost touching her striped kneesocks.

"At night, every place feels like the jungle," Zan whispered ominously. She wrapped her lavender terrycloth robe around her more tightly. The white lace collar on her flannel nightgown peeked out around her neck. "I'm going with you."

"Then you can count me in, too," McGee said, slipping her baseball cap on her head. For some reason she always felt braver with it on.

"Hey!" Gwen put her hands on her hips. "You're not leaving me in this cold old garage by myself, are you? While you're out petting that mutt, I could be in here getting mugged."

"Then we'll all go together," Rocky replied, shining her light on the faces of the girls. "This mission shouldn't be too difficult." Rocky squared her shoulders in her best imitation of her father and ordered, "Now stay in tight formation behind me. On my command, we hit the backyard, grab the basset, and hustle back here in two minutes. Got it?"

"Got it." Everyone nodded bruskly.

Rocky pushed the door open another six inches and squeezed outside. "All right," she whispered to the others. "Fall in."

"Fall in?" Gwen turned to Zan in confusion. "What's that supposed to mean?"

Rocky, who'd already scurried to the corner of the patio, turned back and said impatiently, "It means line up. Now come on! We're wasting time."

"Why didn't you say so in the first place?" Gwen grumbled under her breath as McGee and the others slipped into the backyard. "You know I don't know that military stuff." Gwen shoved her thick body through the gap in the door with a loud "oomph," then huffed and puffed to catch up with the gang.

"Single file," Rocky hissed, grabbing McGee's hand. They quickly formed a human chain and tiptoed across the ground. It was frozen and the dead grass crunched beneath their feet.

"Will you hurry up?" Gwen whispered. "My feet are freezing."

"Don't you have any shoes on?" McGee asked.

"No. Only my socks."

"That's dumb," McGee said. "Why didn't you get your shoes?"

"Because if I had stopped to get my shoes, all of you would have been gone and I would have missed out on this really fun maneuver," Gwen said sarcastically.

Rocky led them across the concrete patio up to the sliding-glass doors. "There's the patio door."

"That's wh-where I h-h-heard him scratching," Mary said through chattering teeth.

"Well, the dog's not here," McGee observed.

"No kidding, Sherlock," Gwen snorted. "He probably just ran away."

"This is a big backyard," Zan whispered, peering out into the darkened yard. "He could be hiding."

"Hoover?" Rocky called softly. "Are you out there?"

They each held their breath and listened.

"He's not answering because that's not his name," Mary said. She clucked her tongue. "Come on, Oscar. That's a good boy."

"O'Rourke!" Gwen cried, cupping her hands around her mouth. "I've got two extra packs of Twinkies with your name on them!"

"Einstein!" Zan called, using the name Hi had given the dog. "Please come out."

"Yo! T-Bone!" McGee shouted. "Get over here *now!*"

"Don't talk to Oscar like that," Mary protested. "He's a very sensitive dog."

"Well, if he's so sensitive, why isn't he answering?" Gwen retorted, hopping from one foot to the other. Her feet were really starting to hurt from the cold. "I mean, we've got five people calling him."

"That's the problem," Rocky said. "He's confused. He doesn't know which person to answer to, so he's just keeping quiet."

A whimper sounded directly behind them. Rocky spun around and aimed the flashlight into the darkness. The beam hit the dog like a tiny spotlight. He was standing near the trunk of a big oak tree in the middle of the yard.

"It's Oscar," Mary Bubnik cried. "But what's the matter with him?"

The dog stood frozen with one paw up, and his tail sticking straight out behind him.

"Come on, boy!" McGee called. "We're over here."

He kept staring straight ahead, whimpering softly.

"Maybe the light has scared him," Zan reasoned. "You know how deer freeze on the highway when headlights shine on them. Try turning off your flashlight."

Rocky flicked off the light and the five girls, still holding hands, inched their way across the lawn toward the dog.

Suddenly the backyard was ablaze with light.

"Halt!" a deep male voice shouted over a bullhorn. "Security police!"

The girls sprang together and clung to each other in terror, blinking out into the glaring searchlights.

"Don't shoot!" Gwen squeaked. "Don't shoot!"

"We're unarmed," Rocky added shakily.

"What the — ?" the voice said. "Why, it's just a bunch of kids."

"Hey, that's my daughter," Rocky heard her father exclaim.

"Uh-oh." Rocky swallowed hard. "I'm in big trouble now."

"Sergeant Garcia, is this your idea of a joke?" the deep voice demanded.

The girls heard the chain-link fence rattle, followed by a heavy thud as Rocky's father hopped into the backyard.

"Sorry, Chief," he called. "I thought I heard something suspicious out here and called for backup."

The sergeant flashed the light on the dog, who was still frozen in point position. Abruptly he turned his back to the tree and dog and yelled, "I guess I was wrong about the noise, Chief. I expect our man has headed for the sewer plant."

"Dad — " Rocky started to say, but her father put his finger to his lips.

"Now you girls get on back to the house," he said in a loud voice, all the while waving his arm above his head in a wide circle. The girls stared at him in bewilderment.

"What's with your dad?" Gwen whispered. "He's acting really weird."

As if in answer to Gwen's question, Sergeant Garcia dropped down beside his daughter and said out of the side of his mouth, "Rochelle! Four point. Into the house. Double time. *Now!*"

Rocky dropped immediately to the ground on all fours and hissed, "You guys, follow me!"

The others, including Gwen, were too startled to question her order. They crawled as fast as they could on their hands and knees back into the garage. Rocky slammed the door shut, and they bolted through the garage into the kitchen. Once inside, she locked the door behind them.

"What was that all about?" McGee asked.

"Dad's onto something," Rocky replied, her eyes shining with excitement. "Let's go see."

They raced into the den and, cracking the curtain across the sliding door, peered through the glass into the backyard.

At least twenty soldiers had circled the big oak tree, their guns at the ready.

"They're not going to shoot Oscar, are they?" Mary Bubnik cried out in horror.

"No way," McGee replied. "They're aiming up into the tree."

"Why?" Gwen asked. "What could be up — ?"

"The tree house!" Rocky exclaimed. "Someone's up in my tree house!"

"Airman Gronkey, you're surrounded," Sergeant Garcia shouted. "Drop your weapon, and come out with your hands up."

A round-faced man with a bald head and wire-rimmed glasses stuck his head out of the tree house window. "D-d-don't shoot," he stammered. "I d-d-don't have a weapon."

The man Sergeant Garcia had called Chief took the bullhorn and ordered, "All right, Gronkey. Now come down with your hands above your head."

The little man shook his head. "No way. First you put a muzzle on your dog."

"Are you kidding?" Sergeant Garcia's boss said, staring at the odd-looking basset. "That mutt?"

"You bet," the prisoner declared. "He's already taken one bite out of my rear end. I'm not going to give him another chance at me."

The policemen shone their flashlights on the dog, who still hadn't budged. A shredded piece of green material was clearly hanging from his mouth.

"Oscar bit the convict!" Mary gasped.

"All right!" Rocky said as she and McGee exchanged high fives.

"What a dog!" Zan said, shaking her head in admiration.

The girls watched Rocky's father walk over to the dog and hold out his hand. "Give it to me."

Without relaxing his point, the dog obediently opened his mouth, and Sergeant Garcia removed the scrap of Airman Gronkey's uniform.

"Well done, boy," Sergeant Garcia said, patting the dog on the head. Then he added, "At ease."

The dog promptly sat down and set to work licking his front paw.

"Are you going to put a leash on that dog?" the escaped man shouted.

"It's all right, Gronkey," Sergeant Garcia shouted back. He grinned down at the hound and said, "He's on voice command. I can control him."

There was a rustle of branches, and then a figure jumped out of the tree house onto the grass. He stood up and raised his hands, blinking nervously. Instantly a swarm of blue uniforms surrounded him.

"Geez Louise, Rocky," McGee exclaimed. "Your dad's a hero."

"He's not the only hero," Rocky replied, pointing out the window. "Look."

As Sergeant Garcia and his men hustled Airman Gronkey toward a waiting patrol car, the prisoner kept looking back over his shoulder nervously. Trotting behind him, his teeth bared menacingly, was Oscar Hoover T-Bone Einstein Slick Eddie O'Rourke.

Chapter Nine

The girls were too excited to go back to sleep and stayed up most of the night talking. It was almost dawn before they finally collapsed onto their sleeping bags. When Mrs. Garcia woke them up at nine-thirty, it felt as if they'd just closed their eyes.

"Rise and shine!" Rocky's mother called from the doorway, flicking the light switch on and off. "Breakfast is ready. Rise and shine!"

"I may rise, but I will never, *ever* shine," Gwen grumbled as she fought her way out of her sleeping bag. "I feel like I've spent the night trapped in a burrito."

"What night?" McGee mumbled, her eyes still shut tightly. "We skipped it and went directly to morning."

Rocky didn't say a word. She pulled herself to a sitting position and stared numbly off in space.

Mrs. Garcia chuckled. "I would have let you girls sleep later, but you have a rehearsal to get to this morning, remember?" She disappeared back into the kitchen.

"Rehearsal?" Gwen buried her head beneath her pillow. "I can't dance. Not in this condition."

"You couldn't dance in any condition," McGee cracked as she struggled with the zipper on her sleeping bag.

Gwen groaned, "That's so funny I forgot to laugh."

Mary Bubnik peeked out from under her blankets. The curls on one side of her head were smashed flat, and the rest of her hair looked like a bird had made its nest in it. "Good morning, everybody," she murmured sleepily.

"What's good about it?" Gwen said shortly.

"Well, for the first time in two weeks, it's sunny outside," Zan replied cheerily. She was busy rolling up her sleeping bag. "We don't have to go to school today, and we don't have to be scared anymore because Einstein and Sergeant Garcia captured the escaped prisoner."

"Hoover! I forgot all about him." Rocky leaped out of her bag and stumbled into the kitchen. "Mom, where's the dog?"

Mrs. Garcia was standing at the stove, flipping pancakes on the griddle. "Don't worry about him," she said. "The pooch is in the garage eating a hero's breakfast of steak and eggs. Your father insisted on it."

Rocky rubbed the sleep from her eyes and grinned. "Dad kind of likes him, doesn't he?"

Her mother smiled. "He *really* likes him. In fact, all he could talk about when he got home this morning was how smart that mutt was."

Rocky came up beside her mother and clutched her arm. "Can we keep him, Mom?" she pleaded softly. "Can we?"

"I'm sorry, honey. But your father and I went over and over it and we just don't see how we can take him with us." She shrugged helplessly. "With five kids, and all of our luggage — there won't be any room in either car."

"So leave my stuff behind," Rocky suggested. "Mom, a dog like this comes along once in a lifetime."

"I know that, dear. But we have to be in Nebraska so soon. . . ." Her mother breathed a heavy sigh. "It was a tough decision, but your father has made up his mind. And you know what that means."

Rocky hung her head. "It means we can't keep him."

"Now I've already been on the phone with Norma McGee," Mrs. Garcia said, "to see if they have room for him at their house."

"What'd she say?" McGee asked, sticking her head in the door.

"She told me she'd have to discuss it with Mr. McGee. She said you already have four dogs, seven cats — "

McGee made a sour face. "Two ducks, five rabbits, and a pair of gerbils. I know. Mom is always saying something has got to go."

"Anyway," Mrs. Garcia continued as she flipped the pancakes onto a large, china platter, "your mother said for you to take him to the ballet studio, and she'll let you know what their decision is after rehearsal."

"Take him to the ballet studio?" Gwen said as she followed Mrs. Garcia and the platter of pancakes to the dining table and sat down. "But what will we do with him while we rehearse?"

Mrs. Garcia poured each girl a tall glass of milk. "Tie him up in the dressing room. He's a good dog. He'll behave."

After breakfast the girls and the basset piled into the Garcia's van. No one said much as Mrs. Garcia drove them to the dance studio. Their sleepless night was starting to take its toll.

The five girls and Oscar Hoover T-Bone Einstein Slick Eddie O'Rourke trudged up the one hundred and two steps in front of the dance building, and then up the three flights of stairs to the studio.

McGee was the first one into the dressing room.

She threw back the curtain and was immediately assaulted by the strong smell of perfume.

"Raid!" McGee coughed and waved her hand in front of her face. "Open a window, it smells like bug spray in here."

Courtney Clay was adjusting her bun in front of the mirror at the dressing table. Alice Wescott was lacing up her ballet shoes on a bench. Page Tuttle sat between the two of them on the floor, her head and body stretched out between her legs all the way to the ground.

"For your information," Courtney huffed, "that is very rare perfume. It's also very expensive."

Page Tuttle glanced up from the floor and gasped when she saw the hound follow the gang into the room. "What is *that?*"

"That is a very rare dog," Gwen replied without missing a beat. "He is also very expensive."

"Make me laugh," Alice Wescott said in her nasal voice. "Who does he belong to?"

The gang looked at each other, but no one could answer. Finally Zan said, "He's between owners."

"He's a disgusting stray," Page declared.

"Get that mongrel out of the dressing room," Courtney snapped. "He's not allowed in here."

"Says who?" Rocky put her hands on her hips and took a threatening step forward. "You?"

"Says Mr. Anton," Courtney replied, shrinking back in fear. She scooted down the row of benches toward the door, keeping as far away from the dog as possible. "And I'm telling."

"Tattletale!" McGee sang out.

As Page and Alice tried to inch past the gang after their leader, the dog let out a low growl.

"Careful, or I'll have Hoover put a couple of runs in your tights," Rocky warned with a grin.

"You keep that vicious beast away from us," Courtney called over her shoulder as the Bunheads ran out of the room.

Rocky dropped to one knee and scratched the dog behind one ear. "Good doggie. You know a Bunhead when you see one, don't you, boy."

The hound replied with a loud "Woof!"

The gang laughed as they put on their dance clothes. Gwen, who didn't like to change clothes in public, hurried behind the standing mirror.

"I don't know why we have to wear these things today," she complained as she struggled to get into her leotard. "All we're going to do is talk."

"Leotards help us look like dancers," Zan explained.

"And we need all the help we can get," McGee said with a giggle.

After Rocky had changed, she tied the free end of the clothesline to the leg of the dressing table. "Wait here, boy," she whispered to the dog. "We'll be right back."

As the girls walked to the big rehearsal studio,

they saw Courtney standing at the front reception desk, whispering into the phone.

"She's probably crying to her mother about the dog," Rocky said in disgust. "What a baby!"

The rehearsal hall was packed with girls of all ages, and everyone was chattering at once. Anton Largo, the silver-haired director of the Deerfield Academy, stood in front of a large blackboard. The tall, slender man was dressed simply, in gray slacks and a white turtleneck.

His partner, Josephine York, was busily copying names onto the blackboard from a list she held in her left hand. Her jet black hair, which she wore coiled in a soft bun at the base of her neck, had dramatic streaks of gray running through it. Miss Jo looked every inch a dancer, from her delicately tapered fingers to the elegant way she carried herself. Most of the students at the Academy were intimidated by Mr. Anton, but they adored Miss Jo.

A tall stack of clothing had been piled onto the floor, and Miss Hamilton, who was the Ballet's wardrobe mistress, was busily snipping off loose threads and tags with a pair of scissors.

"Those must be our costumes," Mary squealed. "Let's sit in front so we can get a better look."

The girls pushed their way through the crowd and sat down cross-legged on the floor just as Miss Jo turned to address the group.

"I'm delighted that so many of you will be joining

us for the Winter Carnival this Saturday," Miss Jo said, clasping her hands in front of her. "It promises to be a spectacular event as well as a lot of fun."

A cheer went up from the beginning class of second- and third-graders.

"Now today we'll be distributing costumes for the parade," Mr. Anton said, stepping forward. "To do this in an orderly fashion, we must maintain silence." He glared severely at the girls who had just cheered. "Miss Jo will call your group by name, and Miss Hamilton will hand you your costume. Remember the order because that will be your place in the parade. There will be no rehearsal. You'll receive your costume today and parade across the lake Saturday."

"Look!" Zan pointed to several green velvet coats with thick fur collars lying on top of the stack of clothes. "Those were from the party scene in *The Nutcracker*."

"I hope we get to wear them," Mary Bubnik whispered back. "They're beautiful."

"The first group is Mr. Anton's advanced technique class," Miss Jo read from her clipboard.

"Too bad," McGee said as she watched the class of older girls step forward and *ooh* and *ah* over their new costumes.

"Don't sweat it," Rocky said. "Look at those neat dresses underneath. They're all different colors of corduroy."

"And they have little fur muffs and hats that

match," Zan added, clapping her hands together in delight.

"Shannon Roy's Tuesday and Thursday class," Miss Jo announced.

"Rats," Gwen muttered under her breath. "Just 'cause we only take class once a week, we're going to get stuck with the ugly ones."

"Oh, don't say that!" Mary Bubnik said. "It's bad luck."

"She's right," McGee added. "Look, there are lots more costumes up there."

The next series of dresses was revealed, and the entire room went silent. They were made out of coarse burlap and had red and green patches sewn on the sleeves and skirts.

"Those are from *The Little Match Girl,*" Zan explained.

"Could have fooled me," Gwen cracked. "They look like rejects from the Goodwill store."

"Wonder what poor suckers will have to wear those," Rocky wondered out loud.

Miss Jo looked up from her clipboard and called out, "Annie Springer's Saturday afternoon class."

"Not fair!" Gwen protested.

"Me and my big mouth," Rocky groaned.

Behind them the gang could hear Courtney and Page complaining, too.

"Well, come on up, girls," Mr. Anton said. "We don't have all day."

Slowly the girls got to their feet and shuffled forward, with the Bunheads right behind them. Just as they reached the front of the room, Miss Hamilton said, "Oh, dear. I seem to have miscounted. There aren't enough costumes for all of you."

"All *right!*" Rocky cried, raising her fist in the air in triumph.

"Give them what you have," Miss Jo suggested, "and the others we can pull from the next group."

Zan saw that the next costumes were embroidered Austrian peasant dresses with puffed sleeves from the *Dracula* ballet. "Quick, step back!" she whispered.

Before they could make a move, Miss Hamilton quickly hung one of the burlap dresses on Rocky's raised fist. "Thank you for volunteering," she said pleasantly.

Rocky was too stunned to respond. Just as quickly the other burlap dresses were distributed among the gang.

Courtney and her friends received the beautiful Austrian peasant dresses. As they headed back to their place, Courtney said in mock sympathy, "Aww. Too bad for you guys."

Rocky bristled and raised her fist. "Too bad for you."

"Attention, please!" Mr. Anton clapped his hands. "Take your costumes to the dressing room and try them on. If you have any problems, report back here and Miss Hamilton will arrange to have them altered."

"These don't need to be altered," Rocky said as the girls trudged toward the door of the studio. "They need to be nuked."

"Maybe they won't fit at all," McGee said, "and then we won't have to wear them."

As Mary Bubnik opened the door, she stopped dead in her tracks. "Oh, no!"

"What?" Gwen asked from the back of the line. "Are they uglier than we thought?"

"No, no, it's Oscar!" Mary cried. "They're taking him away!"

"Who's taking him?" McGee demanded, trying to look over Mary's shoulder.

"Two people in gray uniforms."

"They'd better not!" Rocky shouted, as the girls leaped as one through the door.

The scene that greeted them in the reception area outside the studio was worse than they could have imagined. Two animal control officers had the dog pinned on the floor of the office. Each dog-catcher held a long aluminum pole, with a chain noose at the end which they'd slipped over the dog's neck.

"Pull him over to the door," one of the men shouted to the other, as the basset thrashed his head back and forth in a struggle to escape.

"This dog is not going anywhere," Rocky shouted,

stepping between the two men. "So you take those rotten things off him right this minute."

"Is this your dog?" the man asked, as he struggled to keep control of his pole. His face was flushed bright red from exertion.

Rocky hesitated. "Sort of."

"What do you mean, sort of?" the other dogcatcher asked. "Either he is, or he isn't."

"And if he is," his partner added, "where's his collar and tag?"

"We just got Einstein," Zan explained. "We intend to get tags as soon as possible. So please release him and we'll get him out of here."

"Sorry," the red-faced man said. "We can't do that."

"Why not?" Gwen demanded.

"We received a complaint that this dog bit someone here at the studio," the other officer replied.

"Oscar's never bitten anyone in his life," Mary Bubnik cried indignantly.

The red-faced man narrowed his eyes suspiciously. "I thought you said his name was Einstein."

"It is," Mary replied, blinking her big blue eyes at the dogcatcher. "Oscar Einstein."

The man, still keeping one hand on his pole, reached in his back pocket and pulled out an official-looking pad. "According to a Mrs. Clay, this dog bit her daughter less than an hour ago."

"O'Rourke didn't bite Courtney!" Gwen shouted. "But he *should* have."

"Where is she?" Rocky turned furiously. "I'll bite her myself."

"O'Rourke?" the other guard repeated. "You said this dog's name is Oscar Einstein."

"Well, his full name is T-Bone Oscar Eddie Slick Hoover O'Rourke Einstein," Mary said, ticking the names off on her fingers. "But we all call him — " She paused and looked at her friends. "Um, we all call him . . ."

Zan, who had been looking at a bag of dance supplies leaning against the wall while she listened to Mary recite the names, suddenly blurted out, "Toe Shoe. We all call him Toe Shoe."

The other girls stared at her in confusion.

"Toe Shoe?" Gwen repeated.

Zan nodded. "Yes. **T**-Bone **O**scar **E**ddie **S**lick **H**oover **O**'Rourke **E**instein." She shrugged. "Toe Shoe."

Rocky studied the dog for a moment, then smiled. "Toe Shoe. I like it."

"Well, while you kids are making up names," the red-faced dogcatcher said, "we have to get this mutt out of here."

"And until all charges are dropped," his partner added, "we're going to have to keep this dog at the pound."

Toe Shoe let out a sharp yelp as they dragged him over the threshold into the corridor.

"They're hurting him," Zan cried. "We've got to stop them."

"Don't be scared, Toe Shoe!" McGee called as the dog disappeared down the stairs with the dogcatchers. "We'll save you."

"Poor doggie," Mary Bubnik's eyes welled up with tears. "They're taking him to jail, and he may never get out."

"We'll get him out." Rocky slammed her fist into her palm. "I don't care if I have to drag Courtney to the pound and put her there in his place — he's getting out."

Chapter Ten

The girls sat glumly on the benches of the dressing room, their ugly burlap costumes lying forgotten in a heap on the floor. Meanwhile, Rocky paced back and forth in front of them like an angry cat.

"I say we jump Courtney when she comes through the door," Rocky declared. "Then torture her till she calls the dog pound." Rocky gave the air a karate kick for emphasis.

"I second the motion," Gwen said. "Although torture is too good for the jerk. I think we should just throw her out the window."

"Y'all are sounding so violent," Mary said, shaking her head. "I don't think that's going to get us anywhere."

Zan nodded and stood up. "Mary's right. We have to approach Courtney in a reasonable manner. We'll tell her how much Toe Shoe means to us, and ask her — politely — to call the dog pound."

"What if she says no?" McGee asked.

Zan shrugged. "*Then* we torture her and throw her out the window."

Gwen dug in her ballet bag for a pack of M&M's left over from the slumber party and popped a handful in her mouth. "The question is, what kind of torture?"

"Hammer nails in her ballet slippers," Rocky suggested. "That's good for starters. Then hack off her bun with a chain saw and give her a crew cut."

"Boy, she'd *hate* that," Mary said, with a wicked giggle.

McGee sat straight up in her seat. "She *would* hate that. It's perfect!"

Zan's eyes widened. "Are you seriously suggesting we cut off Courtney's hair?"

"Of course not," McGee replied as she rifled through the pile of costumes on the floor. Several of the caps had wigs sewn right onto them. McGee held up a dark-haired one and grinned slyly. "But we can *pretend* to do it."

"Oh, that's *good,*" Rocky said, catching on. "We'll just act like we're cutting off her bun."

"Then we'll cut off a chunk of this and show it to her," McGee finished.

"She'd have a heart attack," Mary Bubnik warned. "And then we'd be accused of murder."

"Relax, Mary," Gwen said, crunching calmly on her candy as she pawed through her dance bag. "Bunheads don't have heart attacks — they have tantrums." She pulled out a small pair of scissors and handed them to Rocky. "I knew there was a reason I was carrying these around."

"All right!" Rocky snipped the air once or twice with the scissors to test them out, then carefully cut off a lock of the wig.

Mary frowned nervously. "I still don't think it's such a good idea. We'd just get in more trouble."

"Well, the more we just sit here doing nothing," Rocky replied, "the longer Toe Shoe has to sit in the slammer." She put her hands on her hips. "Have you ever seen a dog pound?"

Mary shook her head.

"Well, the dogs stay in these narrow cages with cement floors. There are a dozen other dogs already in there, and they're all barking at once. Then once a day the keepers hose the cages down and toss some food in."

Mary's eyes widened. "It sounds terrible!"

Zan nodded sadly. "It's truly awful."

"We've got to save Toe Shoe!" Mary cried, leaping to her feet. "Right away."

"So are you with us?" Rocky asked, sticking out her hand.

"I'm with you!" Mary cried, putting hers on top.

"Good," McGee called softly, pointing at the curtained entrance to the dressing room. "Because here comes Courtney."

Courtney held her peasant costume proudly out in front of her.

"Pretty costume, Courtney," Rocky said, as she and the others closed in around her. "Too bad you won't be able to wear it."

Courtney clutched the dress to her chest. "What do you mean?"

"I don't think they'll let bald ballerinas in the parade," Rocky explained, as she moved towards Courtney.

"Bald?" Courtney asked in confusion. "What do you mean?"

Rocky took a hold of Courtney's bun and held the pair of scissors in front of her startled eyes. "It's time for your haircut!"

"Rocky!" McGee hissed, as the rest of the gang huddled together, acting shocked. "What do you think you're doing?"

Courtney struggled to kick Rocky in the shin. "Let go of my hair!"

"Kicking won't save your hair, Courtney," Rocky said, snipping the scissors open and closed. "There's only one way you can keep from becoming a bald Bunhead."

"How?" Courtney asked, not daring to move her head.

"Call the dog pound and tell the truth — that you lied. Tell them our dog did *not* bite you, and you want him released *immediately*."

"No!" Courtney said, her eyes flashing with anger.

Rocky sighed reluctantly. "Okay, then. You've forced me to start trimming."

"You wouldn't dare!" Courtney cried out in horror.

"Oh, wouldn't I?" Rocky replied. She tugged on Courtney's bun and snipped the scissors at the same time. Then she held up the lock of dark hair from the wig in front of Courtney's astonished face.

"She actually did it," Gwen gasped, pretending to be amazed.

"Now we'll take a little off the sides," Rocky said, leaning forward.

"Rocky, stop!" Mary Bubnik cried dramatically. "If you cut off all of Courtney's hair, it will take *years* and *years* to grow back."

"That's right," McGee added. "She can kiss her dancing career bye-bye."

"That's not true," Zan protested. "What's hair got to do with being a ballerina?"

"Have you ever seen a prima ballerina without a bun?" Gwen asked, folding her arms. "I rest my case."

"Rocky Garcia, I'm calling the police and have you

put in jail for the rest of your life if you don't stop it right now," Courtney cried, kicking at Rocky.

"I can't stop," Rocky cried hysterically. "I want my dog back. And if I have to cut off all of your hair, and Page's, and Alice's hair, and shred their costumes — I'll do it."

"She's out of control," Zan whispered to Courtney in a low, worried voice. "There's no stopping her when she's like this."

Rocky waved the scissors wildly above her head, doing her best mad scientist laugh. "Shall I cut some more?" she whispered, snipping the scissors in front of Courtney's nose.

"No, stop!" Courtney shouted. "I'll call the pound, I promise!"

Rocky nodded at McGee and Gwen. "Escort Courtney to the phone in the office."

Courtney bolted from Rocky and hid behind the two girls. "She's a maniac. Keep her away from me!" McGee and Gwen quickly ushered Courtney toward the curtain.

When they left, Zan whispered. "Do you think that was a little harsh?"

Rocky cocked her head. "What? Pretending to cut her hair? She may have gotten a little scared, but think of Toe Shoe. He's in jail and he's *really* scared — for his life."

Moments later, Courtney and the others returned. But McGee and Gwen were not smiling.

"Bad news," Gwen said. "The pound won't let us have Toe Shoe."

"Didn't Courtney tell them she lied?" Rocky asked.

Courtney, who had picked up her costume, moved quickly to the mirror of the dressing room, feeling her hair. "Of course I told them. They just don't believe that he's your dog." She peered at her hair from all angles and finally stood up. "I knew you wouldn't really cut my hair. You're too much of a chicken." Courtney stuck out her tongue. "So there!"

Rocky lunged for Courtney, but McGee stopped her. "She's not worth the trouble."

Rocky sat down heavily on the bench. "Now what do we do?"

"We've got to convince them he's ours," Zan explained.

"How?"

Zan sighed. "An adult has to accompany us to the pound. Then we have to pay for rabies and distemper shots, and buy him a dog tag."

"How much does all this cost?" Mary Bubnik asked.

"Thirty-five dollars," Gwen replied glumly. "Even if I didn't eat lunch for the rest of the year, I still wouldn't be able to save Toe Shoe."

"Besides, that wouldn't be in time," Rocky said.

"What do you mean, not in time?" Mary asked in a small voice.

"What she means," Gwen said bluntly, "is that, if

no one claims an animal within a month, they have to get rid of it."

Mary swallowed hard. "You mean, permanently?"

Rocky nodded. "Permanently."

"This is terrible," McGee exploded. "I'm going to talk to my parents and tell them we *have* to save Toe Shoe."

"Everyone else's parents have said no," Zan said. "Your mom and dad are our only hope."

"This can't wait another minute," McGee said, slamming her baseball cap over her braids. "I'm going home right now."

"But what about our costumes?" Mary asked. "We're supposed to try them on."

"Who cares about them?" Gwen said. "No matter how we wear them, they're going to look awful."

"Gwen's right," Rocky said. "Let's just hang 'em up and leave a note saying they're fine."

"And then what?" Zan asked.

McGee was already out of the dressing room when she called over her shoulder, "Then we save Toe Shoe!"

Chapter Eleven

That night Rocky was in her room packing when she heard the phone ring in the kitchen. "I'll get it," she shouted as she ran down the hall. When Rocky got to the kitchen, her brother Michael was standing by the ringing phone, grinning mischievously.

"I'm expecting a call," Rocky explained, reaching for the phone. "I'm sure it's for me."

"But what if it's not?" Michael said, holding it out of her reach.

"Give me that!" Rocky yanked the phone out of his hand and dragged it under the kitchen table, as far away from her brother as the cord would allow.

"Sergeant Garcia's residence," she said politely into the receiver.

"Rocky, it's me, McGee," a miserable voice said. "I've got bad news."

"Your parents won't let you take Toe Shoe," Rocky said, knowing the answer.

"Right. They say we have too many pets, and I don't take care of them as it is."

"But didn't you explain that he could be on Death Row?"

"I tried everything. I even promised to do the dishes for the next two months, and mow the lawn all summer, but it didn't work. My dad said if this dog is so great, he's sure to find a home."

"I guess you didn't tell them what he looks like," Rocky said.

"No," McGee confessed. "I was saving that for later."

Rocky leaned her head back against the wall and moaned. "This is terrible, McGee! You were our last hope."

"I called Mary and Zan to see if they would try to retalk their parents into taking him, but it didn't work," McGee said. "And nobody had any ideas exept Zan."

Rocky sat up. "What did she say we should do?"

"Oh, you know her," McGee said. "Sometimes she gets carried away with her Tiffany Truenote mystery books and thinks she's a detective, too."

"What did Zan say?" Rocky repeated.

"She said we should go down to the dog pound and try to spring him ourselves."

Rocky, who was sprawled out under the kitchen table, leaped up in excitement and banged her head. "Ow!"

"That's what I said," McGee went on. "I mean, a bunch of fifth- and sixth-graders breaking into the dog pound? Get real."

"I think it's a great idea!" Rocky said, getting to her feet.

"Rocky, are you nuts?" McGee shouted through the phone. "How are we going to do it? And what are we going to do with Toe Shoe if we do rescue him?"

"Those are little details we can work out later," Rocky replied confidently.

"Little!" McGee exclaimed. "I think you've definitely started to slip over the edge."

"McGee," Rocky cut in impatiently. "Aren't you worried about Toe Shoe?"

"Of course I am," McGee retorted. "But I'm also worried about me. Okay, so he's in a cell with a cold cement floor and just one meal a day. He's used to that. I'm not. I'd starve."

"We won't get caught. Not if we plan it right." Rocky chewed on the edge of one fingernail. "I won't be able to get back into town till Saturday. Do you think Toe Shoe will be okay until then?"

"I think so," McGee said. "Maybe we can get Zan or Mary Bubnik to visit him, since they live in town."

"In the meantime," Rocky said. "I'll work out the details. And on Saturday, we hit the pound!"

The following Saturday the gang met in the parking lot outside the Deerfield Animal Control Shelter. Because the Winter Carnival Ice Extravaganza was to start at noon, they had agreed to wear their costumes.

"Who would have thought these dresses would be so huge?" Mary Bubnik said, peering woefully at the group. They each wore their costumes over their heavy parkas, which gave them a roly-poly look.

"We should have talked to Miss Hamilton, the seamstress," McGee said, shaking her head. "She would have taken in these things."

"We look like potato people," Gwen complained, pulling the cap that matched her dress down over her ears. "Even Zan looks round. That's a miracle."

Mary stepped back and giggled. "When y'all stand close together like that, you look like one giant burlap bag with little doll heads sticking out of it."

"I feel like one giant bag," McGee grumbled as she tugged on the rope of the old sled that rested on the ground behind her. "To top it off, we didn't even decorate our sled. Now the Bunheads will win the contest."

"Look," Rocky said gruffly, "what is more important? Rescuing Toe Shoe, or putting some streamers on a dumb sled?"

"Rescuing Toe Shoe," McGee admitted. She kicked at a clump of grimy snow in the parking lot. "But I still hate it that the Bunheads are going to win."

"We *all* hate it," Rocky said, her dark eyes flashing. "But we have an important mission to accomplish, right?"

McGee grinned. "Right."

"What's that awful smell?" Mary asked, wrinkling her nose. She sniffed at the air, following the scent right to Gwen's blue corduroy bag. "It's your dance bag!" Mary cried, pinching her nose. "P.U.! What's in there?"

Gwen shoved her glasses up on her nose. "You told me to bring the bait. So I bought pet food."

"But why can we smell it? What's it in?" Zan asked.

"I couldn't very well bring ten cans and a can opener. I'd be opening cans for days," Gwen replied. "I bought the stuff yesterday, opened it up, and poured it into a plastic bag. Then I put it in my dance bag and hid it under the bed." She opened the bag to take a whiff and her head jerked back in shock. "Whew! Maybe it got a little too close to the heater."

"It smells like dog *and* cat food," Zan said.

"It is," Gwen replied. "Kilmer's had a big sale on cat food."

"Well, just to be on the safe side, don't go near the desk when we get inside the pound," Rocky instructed. "We wouldn't want them to smell you and blow the whole operation." She consulted the clipboard she had brought. "Now, Mary, did you get the supplies?"

Mary nodded and pulled several items out of her pocket. "One leash. One collar. And one dog tag."

Gwen squinted at the collar. "That's not a dog tag. That's a heart from a charm bracelet."

"So?" Mary retorted. "It looks like a tag."

"Not up close, it doesn't." Gwen grabbed hold of the little silver heart and read the inscription out loud. " 'For our little Mary — congratulations on becoming a Brownie.' "

Mary giggled. "My grandparents gave me that five years ago."

Gwen rolled her eyes. "Oh, brother."

Rocky consulted her checklist again. "Now let's go over the plan one more time. We tell the person at the desk that our mother is waiting for us in the car, that she wants us to pick out a few dogs, and that she'll then come inside and help us choose the best one."

Mary repeated Rocky's words softly under her breath as she spoke them.

"Then on my signal — "

"What's the signal?" Mary cut in. "I forgot."

"Rocky yells 'chow time!' " Zan answered.

"Oh, right." Mary nodded her head so hard her curls bounced. "That's when Gwen throws the bait to the dogs."

"Thus creating a diversion," Zan continued, "so we can rescue Toe Shoe."

"I hope this works," Gwen said dubiously.

McGee dismissed Gwen's fears with a wave of her hand. "Don't worry, it's gonna be a cinch."

"Okay." Rocky tucked her clipboard under her arm and looked at her friends. "Inside that building is a great dog and our friend."

The others looked solemnly up at the low concrete building. It had a bright yellow door with a picture of two puppies painted on it, but to the gang it looked like the most awful, impenetrable prison in the world.

"Ready?" Rocky asked.

"Ready," the others chorused. They marched up the sidewalk in single file and pushed open the bright yellow door.

A heavyset man with a thin, dark moustache was sitting behind the desk at the pound, reading a newspaper. He seemed totally oblivious to the hundreds of dogs barking in the next rooms.

Rocky stepped up to the desk and cleared her throat. "Excuse me. We're here to pick out a dog."

"Sorry," the man said without looking up. "We don't give dogs to kids. Only responsible adults."

"Yeah, well, our mother's waiting in the car outside," McGee said.

The man glanced at them over the top of his paper.

"As soon as we pick the one we want, Mom will come in and pay for him," Zan added.

"*All* of you have the same mother?" the man asked, raising a skeptical eyebrow at Zan.

"We were adopted," Gwen said quickly.

The man hesitated for a moment, eyeing their strange outfits, then shrugged. "Go through that door," he said, gesturing over his shoulder with his thumb. "Dogs in the front cages. Cats in the back."

"Thanks a lot, mister," Mary Bubnik said cheerfully, but the man was already back reading his paper.

"That was easier than I thought," Rocky whispered.

"Let's not press our luck," Gwen replied as they hurried through the door. "We'd better — "

She was cut off by the deafening sound of hundreds of barking dogs.

Mary Bubnik covered her ears. "This is awful. Poor Toe Shoe must be terrified."

Rocky nodded. "Let's split up and find him. Zan, you and McGee take the far aisle. And Gwen and I will look over here."

"What should I do?" Mary Bubnik asked.

"Go ask the man at the desk if we can look at a few dogs," Rocky said to Mary Bubnik. "They're supposed to let you do it."

Mary nodded and hurried back through the swinging door.

Rocky and Gwen moved slowly past cages filled with German shepherd mixes, shaggy retrievers, and tiny terriers. One cage had ten black-and-white puppies. As they passed by, the dogs wagged their tiny tails and hopped up and down excitedly against the chain-link walls.

"Poor guys," Rocky said as she and Gwen waited by the cage. "I wish we could take them all out of here."

"All but that one," Gwen said, pointing at a pit bull that was all by himself in another cage. "He can stay here as long as he likes." The dog bared his jaws and hurled himself against the chain-link gate, growling viciously.

"He must have heard you," Rocky said, flinching.

Zan popped out at the end of the aisle. "We found Toe Shoe!"

The girls made a wide arc around the cage of the snarling dog and hurried to join their friends.

Zan and McGee were standing by the far cage. Ten motley dogs clustered around the gate, pressing their noses through the fence and yapping for all they were worth. Sitting quietly all by himself in the far corner was the mournful hound, staring at the ground.

"Toe Shoe!" Rocky cried.

The hound thumped his tail twice in recognition, then hung his head.

"He looks terrible," Zan said.

"He must really be depressed," McGee murmured.

"Well, wouldn't you be, after spending an entire week in jail?" Gwen replied.

Rocky knelt down and snapped her fingers. "Come here, boy," she said softly.

Toe Shoe pulled himself to his feet and pushed his way through the crowd of barking dogs. Rocky pressed her fingers on the cage and Toe Shoe stuck his nose through the links and touched her hand. "His nose is all hot!" she cried. "He must be sick."

"We've got to hurry and get him out of here," McGee said.

"What's taking Mary so long?" Gwen asked.

Just then the door to the office swung open and Mary came through with the attendant. She led him to where her friends were. "We'd like to see a little black-and-white fuzzy one," she was saying. "And the one that looks like a golden retriever."

"That big one in back?" the man asked, jangling a big ring of keys that was attached to his belt by a thin chain.

"Umm, I'd like to see him, too," Mary said. "And bring his friend, the one that's missing an ear. Oh, and the one that looks like Benji."

"I told her to ask to see a few dogs, not the entire kennel," Rocky muttered.

"Is that all?" the man demanded impatiently.

Rocky cleared her throat loudly. "And we'd also like to take a look at the one that looks like a basset hound."

The man looked up in surprise. "That ugly mutt?"

"He's not ugly, and he's not a mutt," Zan huffed indignantly.

"Well, to each his own," the attendant grumbled. "That's six dogs you want to see. Now where's your mother?"

"She'll be right here," Rocky said. "She just wanted to give us a few minutes to meet the dogs."

"Okay." The man unlocked the gate and squeezed inside. The dogs clambered all over him, trying to get his attention. "Get away from me," he yelled. He looped a rope leash around each dog's neck and led them out one by one to the cement walk between the cages. Zan and Mary petted and fussed over the dogs as they came out.

"Don't forget this one," McGee reminded him, pointing to Toe Shoe.

"How could I forget a face like that?" the man replied. "Get out of here, Muttly," he said, shoving Toe Shoe forward. Then he turned to the girls and said, "You've got five minutes."

The man sat down on a stool near the back door and crossed his arms.

"Okay, Gwen, open your bag," Rocky said under her breath.

Gwen unzipped the bag and a terrible smell filled the air.

McGee made a face. "It smells awful."

"They don't think so." Gwen pointed to the dogs who had gathered around her, nudging the bag with their noses and whining.

"Okay, let's move closer to the front door," Rocky whispered. "Then toss the meat out behind us."

"And when the guy goes to break up the dogs," McGee added with a grin, "we're out of here."

The girls inched slowly back toward the swinging door, making a big show of *ooh-ing* and *ah-ing* over the dogs. Just before they got there, two more animal control workers stepped into the concrete walkway from the back of the building.

Zan looked up in shock. "Aren't those the guys — ?"

She didn't have time to finish her sentence. The red-faced man saw them and his eyes widened in surprise. "Hey, it's those kids from that ballet school," he shouted. "What are you doing here?"

"We've come to get a dog," Zan declared.

"Oh, yeah?" the other man said. "Where are your parents?"

"They're — *she's* outside," Rocky replied.

"You know these kids?" the man on the stool asked.

The red-faced man nodded. "Yeah, they tried to stop us from taking the basset mutt there."

"What are you doing with all those other dogs?" his partner demanded.

The girls backed away nervously as the two men strode toward them. Finally Rocky shouted, "Chow time!"

The signal caught Gwen so much by surprise that she tossed her bag straight in the air. It hit the ground directly in front of her and all of the dogs, including Toe Shoe, dove for it.

"Get Toe Shoe!" McGee shouted.

"I can't," Gwen cried, trying to dart her hand in between the dogs lunging hungrily for the bag. "He's eating the food, too."

Rocky grabbed Toe Shoe's tail and pulled for all she was worth. He came sliding out of the pile, the dance bag firmly grasped in his teeth. "Pick him up, you guys!"

The gang sprang into action. Zan and Mary got Toe Shoe around the middle, while McGee picked up his hindquarters. They heaved him up and the dogs leaped up all around them, trying to get at the meat in the bag.

"What are you doing with that dog?" the red-faced attendant shouted. "Put him down!"

"No way!" Rocky shouted back.

"Get 'em," the other attendant ordered. The three men ran to the wall and pulled down the long poles the gang had seen them use to nab Toe Shoe at the Academy.

Suddenly there was a loud crash from the next aisle.

"What was that?" one of the men shouted.

The huge pit bull came barreling around the corner, heading straight for the clump of girls and dogs.

"It's Diesel!" the red-faced man cried. "He's broken out of his cage."

"Look out!" his partner cried. All three workers dropped their poles and clambered up the chain-link cages as Diesel hurtled past them, snapping at everything in sight.

For a moment all the girls, including the dogs, froze in terror as they watched the horrible beast charge at them. Then Gwen stuck her hand in the bag and tossed a large handful of dog food in the dog's path. He caught it in midair.

"Throw him some more," Rocky urged.

Gwen jerked the bag out of Toe Shoe's mouth and hurled another hunk of food at the dog. He paused for just a second to shake it around before swallowing.

"Throw him the whole bag," McGee shouted.

"Are you kidding?" Gwen retorted. "This is my dance bag. I'm not going to — "

With a roar Diesel charged again, and Gwen threw the bag at him with all her might. "It's all yours!"

Diesel leaped on the bag with a fury, tearing it to

shreds while the other dogs clustered around him, hoping to pick up any bits that he missed.

"Out the door!" McGee shouted.

"Double time!" Rocky added.

The girls hustled Toe Shoe out through the office into the parking lot.

"Now what?" Mary Bubnik asked.

"The park's across the street," McGee said, pointing with her mitten. "And Deerfield Lake's just beyond that tall clump of trees."

"Grab the sled and we'll go cross-country to the Winter Carnival Ice Extravaganza," Rocky said. "If we hurry, we should get there just in time for the parade."

Toe Shoe and the girls made a run for the park. Behind them they could hear the yellow door bang open and a voice shout, "There they go! Follow them!"

Chapter Twelve

The parade was just getting under way when the girls reached Deerfield Lake. The Civic Orchestra was on the bandshell bordering the lake, playing "The Blue Danube" waltz. Crowds of people lined the shore, cheering the participants. Miss Jo and Mr. Anton, both wearing heavy wool overcoats, were running up and down the line of dancers, giving last-minute instructions.

"I think one of those dogcatchers is still following us," McGee called, glancing back over her shoulder. "Look."

The red-faced man was striding toward them through the trees, his green uniform flashing between the bare tree trunks.

Rocky finished tying her long scarf around Toe Shoe's neck and hurriedly pulled the dog toward the water's edge. "Mingle with the crowd," she instructed. "He'll never be able to find us."

"You've got to be kidding," Gwen said, gasping for breath. "With us dressed like the Potato People, he'll spot us in a second."

"Then everyone take off her costume," Zan shouted, as she struggled to remove hers. It hooked in the back and she couldn't quite reach the zipper.

"There you are!" Mr. Anton's deep voice bellowed from behind them. "Get in your place, girls. You're holding up the parade."

"What place?" Mary Bubnik asked, blinking her big blue eyes at the long, uneven line of costumed dancers. There were sleds covered with brightly colored crepe paper flowers, others decorated with snowflakes made out of gold and silver tinsel. Many of the dancers' mothers were making last-minute adjustments to their daughters' costumes. It was hard to see any order to the gathering at all.

Mr. Anton checked the clipboard. "You are between Miss Roy's class, and the rest of the girls in your class."

"Oh, right," Gwen grumbled. "The cute corduroy dresses with the matching muffs, and the little green Austrian outfits."

"I see Courtney," Zan said, standing up on her

tiptoes. "She's standing by that huge sleigh over there."

The sleigh was painted gold and red, with plush green velvet seats and cushions with golden tassels. Pots of brilliant white and red poinsettias hung from either side of the front, and a big red velvet bow draped off the back.

"That looks like the one that was in Baumgartner's window," Mary Bubnik said, a perplexed look on her face.

"It *is* the one from Baumgartner's," a dancer dressed like a candy cane replied. "Mrs. Clay rented it for the parade."

"That doesn't seem fair," Mary Bubnik protested.

"Hurry up!" Mr. Anton interrupted, pushing the girls forward. He was looking at his clipboard and didn't notice Toe Shoe. "Miss Roy's class is already on the ice."

Two of the older girls stepped onto the frozen lake and, after crossing their arms and holding hands, glided forward on their skates in long graceful strides. The rest of their class followed in matching pairs, skating in perfect time to the music.

Gwen shoved her glasses up on her nose and muttered, "They must have practiced their skating."

"How are we supposed to get across the ice?" Rocky demanded of Mr. Anton. "McGee is the only one who has skates."

"What?" Mr. Anton flipped through his pages on

his pad. "I thought you had a sled entry for the contest."

"We have a sled," Gwen said simply. "But it's not entering any contest. It's just a plain, ordinary — "

"Fine." Mr. Anton pushed the girls closer to the edge of the frozen lake. "Just get on it, and go."

"We'd better do something quick," McGee muttered, checking over her shoulder to see where the animal control officer was. "He's gaining on us."

Rocky grabbed the sled from McGee and tossed it onto the ice. "Get on!" she ordered.

"All of us?" Gwen eyed the tiny sled dubiously. "We'll never fit."

"Don't ask questions, just do it!" Rocky sounded just like her father, and the girls clambered onto the sled. Rocky, Zan, Gwen, and Mary Bubnik knelt on the edges of the sled, their arms wrapped tightly around each other.

McGee swung her hockey skates off her shoulder and, after kicking off her boots, slipped them on her feet. When she looked back up after lacing them, McGee couldn't help giggling.

"What's so funny?" Gwen mumbled. Her face was buried in the burlap shoulder of Rocky's costume.

"You *do* look like one giant bag of toys," McGee said with a grin.

"Well, I'm so thrilled to hear that," Gwen said sarcastically. She winced and added, "Let's get a move on. My knees are already starting to hurt."

McGee grabbed the end of Toe Shoe's scarf and led him to the ice. "Okay, boy, you've got to do this, or it's back to the slammer for you."

Toe Shoe seemed to understand what she was saying and followed McGee onto the ice without hesitation. His front paws slipped, but he quickly regained his balance and soon was standing firmly on all fours. He looked up at her expectantly.

"Wrap the sled rope around his shoulders," Rocky instructed. "Then he can pull us."

"He can try," Gwen muttered, as McGee looped the rope around the dog and fastened it securely.

"Hey, you brats," the red-faced man shouted as he burst through the edge of the crowd lining the shore. "Give that dog back!"

"There's no turning back now!" McGee charged onto the ice and spun to face the dog. "Come on, Toe Shoe, you can do it."

Toe Shoe dug his head down and, with a mighty heave, jerked the sled forward just as the angry dogcatcher reached the edge of the ice.

"He's doing it!" Mary Bubnik squealed as they moved off into the parade. "Toe Shoe is pulling us."

McGee skated backwards ahead of them all, making sure the overloaded sled didn't tip over as it glided across the ice. With so many bodies clinging to it, she couldn't even see the metal runners. "I can't get over how much you guys really look like a sack of presents."

A cheer went up as they passed the first crowd of spectators.

"See?" McGee cried, doing a twirl under the scarf. "They think so, too."

Upon hearing the encouraging shouts, Toe Shoe raised his head proudly and began to trot in time to the music. That prompted another cheer from the shore.

"They love us!" McGee called back over her shoulder. She had positioned herself in an *arabesque* and was gliding forward on one skate, tipping her hat to the crowd. "We're a hit!"

"Great!" Rocky moaned. "Just great."

"What's the matter?" Mary Bubnik asked, waving with one hand at the cheering bystanders. "Isn't this what we wanted?"

"What we wanted was to get away from the dogcatcher and not be noticed," Rocky replied. "Look behind us."

The red-faced man was gingerly making his way across the ice after them. But at every other step, his shiny black boots slipped out from under him and he fell. Finally the man gave up trying to stand and followed them on his hands and knees, raising loud hoots of laughter from the spectators.

"This is truly terrible," Zan said. "We've got that

awful dogcatcher behind us, and look what's waiting for us on the shore."

"I can't see," Rocky mumbled from the middle of the huddle. "What is it?"

Gwen squinted at the grandstand area near the front of the band shell. Three men in dark blue uniforms stood along the shoreline, calmly waiting for the sled to near them. "Oh, no, it's the police."

McGee and Toe Shoe were oblivious to the trouble ahead. Instead, McGee showed off all of her best skating moves, twirling and leaping energetically across the ice. Toe Shoe tried to match each new step, tossing his head playfully in time to the music. He even mixed in a gallop or two with his trot.

An icy breeze blew across the lake, and the girls clung closer to each other. After a minute, Rocky said in a muffled voice, "When we reach the shore, and they arrest us, and take Toe Shoe back to the pound, we probably won't get a chance to talk." She cleared her throat roughly. "So I just want to say I'm going to miss you guys. I also want to say I'm sorry 'cause you'll probably get thrown out of the Deerfield Academy of Dance for wrecking their parade."

"I don't care if I ever dance again," Mary Bubnik said, biting back her tears. "It won't be the same without you, Rocky."

Zan swallowed hard. "You have to promise to write and come visit. I don't think I could bear the thought that we wouldn't see you again."

Gwen tried to make light of the situation, but there was a catch in her voice as she said, "Look on the bright side. Maybe we *will* get to be together after all. In prison."

Rocky and the others laughed, but the tears springing to their eyes weren't from the cold wind. They hugged each other even tighter as McGee led Toe Shoe up to the shore.

Before the sled ran aground, the three men in uniform stepped forward. One lifted McGee off the ice. The other grabbed the scarf attached to Toe Shoe, and the third took hold of the sled and pulled it up to the shoreline.

Rocky started talking a mile a minute as she struggled to get herself out of the huddle. "This was all my fault. I suggested we break into the dog pound, and it was my idea to swipe the dog. But I love Toe Shoe, and I couldn't bear to think what those dogcatchers might do to him. So don't blame any of the gang, they were forced to go along with me, and — "

"At ease, partner," a familiar voice interrupted with a chuckle. "If you hadn't rescued him, I would have."

Rocky's eyes widened and she nearly fell back onto the sled. "Dad? What are you doing here?"

A broad grin spread across Sergeant Garcia's face. "I've been looking for you. I have some good news."

"We're not going to be arrested?" Rocky asked.

"No." He put his hands on his hips and frowned. "However, we do have to have a little discussion about taking matters into your own hands."

"What's the good news?" Rocky asked, quickly changing the subject.

"I got a promotion." Her father tapped his sleeve with pride. Several new stripes had been added to his military insignia. "You are now looking at Senior Master Sergeant Garcia."

"Oh, Dad, that — that's wonderful." Rocky hugged her father, burying her face in his coat to keep her tears from showing. She knew that with his new promotion, any chance of her family staying in Ohio had been wiped out.

"*And* — " Sergeant Garcia continued, "I've been chosen to head the new MWD unit."

"MWD?" Rocky looked up in confusion. "What's that mean?"

Sergeant Garcia leaned over and scratched Toe Shoe behind the ear. "Military Working Dogs. After Toe Shoe's good work last Sunday, the Chief thought that Curtiss-Dobbs could use a canine corps."

"Curtiss-Dobbs?" Rocky leaned back and searched her father's face. "Does that mean we don't have to move?"

Her father nodded. "Unpack your bags. We're staying."

The rest of the gang, who'd been listening intently,

sprang off the sled with a cheer. Wrapping their arms around each other, they hopped happily up and down on the ice. Toe Shoe leaned back his head and let loose with a loud, "Ba-*roo!*"

The sound made all the girls stop cheering.

"Toe Shoe," Rocky said. "What's going to happen to him?"

"I'll take that mutt," a voice cried angrily. They looked up to see the dogcatcher, who'd crawled the entire length of the lake on his hands and knees, pull himself stiffly to his feet. "I want you girls to know that you are in a lot of trouble!"

Toe Shoe lowered his head and, baring his teeth, gave a low warning growl.

"At ease, boy," Sergeant Garcia said, patting the dog on the head. "I'll handle this one." Taking Rocky by the hand, Sergeant Garcia stepped up to the dogcatcher and said, "My daughter acted a little prematurely when she went to the pound this morning. But I can assure you, this is our dog, and we'll pay the release fee."

"This mutt is *really* your dog?" the man asked, squinting one eye at Rocky's father.

Sergeant Garcia nodded briskly and squeezed Rocky's hand.

"Then you don't need to pay a release fee. However, you do have to get him a tag." The man looked at the little heart charm dangling from Toe Shoe's collar and added, "And for your information, girls, *our* tags are orange and shaped like a dog biscuit."

"See?" Gwen hissed at Mary. "I told you no one would think that was a real dog tag."

"Who cares?" Mary Bubnik giggled. "Rocky's staying, Toe Shoe's got a home, and we're not going to be arrested."

"Well!" Sergeant Garcia rubbed his hands together. "This calls for a celebration. Any idea where we can get a nice warm cup of hot chocolate?"

"Hi Lo's!" the girls shouted at once.

"Then let's go." Sergeant Garcia draped one arm over Rocky's shoulder, and clucked his tongue at Toe Shoe, who stood up at attention.

"Wait, I have to take off my costume." Gwen tugged at the zipper of her burlap costume. "If I spend another second in this potato sack, I think I'll scream."

"Not so fast!" Mr. Anton came running up to them, his clipboard under his arm. "You must have your costumes on for the picture."

"Why would anyone want our picture?" Mary Bubnik asked, "when there are so many more beautiful costumes?" She gestured at the parade of dancers and sleds still filing past the shore.

"But don't you know?" Mr. Anton exclaimed.

"Know what?" McGee asked.

"The judges have awarded you second place in the sled contest."

"But we didn't even decorate our sled," Rocky said.

"Yes, you did," Mr. Anton replied. "With your costumed bodies. And your dog. The judges gave you extra points for originality."

"Second place!" Gwen shouted from inside her costume. She'd managed to pull it halfway over her head and gotten stuck there. "Who got first? Courtney?"

Mr. Anton shook his head. "No, her group was disqualified because their sleigh was rented from Baumgartner's. First place went to the snowflake entry."

"How do you like that?" McGee said with a laugh. "We were beaten out by a bunch of flakes."

"What does second place win?" Gwen asked, finally popping her head out of the dress.

"Your photograph in the newspaper," Mr. Anton replied.

"That's a prize?" Gwen scoffed. "Having thousands of people see us dressed like Mr. and Mrs. Potato Head?"

"Well, as far as I'm concerned, we got the best prize of all," Mary Bubnik declared, as the girls knelt around Rocky and Toe Shoe in front of the stage for their picture. "We got to keep our friend Rocky."

McGee draped her arm over Rocky's shoulder. "It just shows you that no one, not the Bunheads, or even the United States Air Force, can break up our friendship."

"That's right." Rocky stuck out her hand between them as she smiled at the camera. "It's one for all — "

The other girls put their hands on top of hers, and chorused, "And all for one!"

As the flash went off, Toe Shoe placed his paw on top of their hands and let loose a joyous, "Ba-*roooooooo!*"